*"I don't have to be g[...]
to win. In the end, A[...]
The rest…the rest doesn't matter."*

"And you'll do anything to win?"

"Anything," Zafar said.

Ana believed him. There was no doubt. The way he said it, so dark and sure and certain, sent a shiver through her body, down into her bones. And yet it didn't repel her. It didn't make her want to run. Perversely, it almost made her want to get closer.

The shock of fear that ran through her body was electric. It sent ripples of warning through her body, showers of sparks that sent crackling heat along her veins.

She felt like a child standing before a fire. Fascinated and awed by the warmth, knowing there was something that might make it all dangerous, but not having any real concept of the damage it could do.

Even having that moment of clarity, she didn't draw back. She took a step toward him.

All about the author...
Maisey Yates

MAISEY YATES knew she wanted to be a writer even before she knew what it was she wanted to write.

At her first job she was fortunate enough to meet her very own tall, dark and handsome hero, who happened to be her boss, and promptly married him and started a family. It wasn't until she was pregnant with her second child that she found her very first Harlequin Presents® book in a local thrift store—by the time she'd reached the happily ever after, she had fallen in love. She devoured as many as she could get her hands on after that, and she knew that these were the books she wanted to write.

She started submitting, and nearly two years later, while pregnant with her third child, she received The Call from her editor—at the age of twenty-three she had sold her first manuscript to the Harlequin Presents® line, and she was very glad that the good news didn't send her into labor!

She still can't quite believe she's blessed enough to see her name on not just any book, but on her favorite books.

Maisey lives with her supportive, handsome, wonderful, diaper-changing husband and three small children, across the street from her parents and the home she grew up in, in the wilds of southern Oregon. She enjoys the contrast of living in a place where you might wake up to find a bear on your back porch, then walk into your home office to write stories that take place in exotic, urban locales.

Other titles by Maisey Yates available in ebook:

A HUNGER FOR THE FORBIDDEN
HIS RING IS NOT ENOUGH
THE COUPLE WHO FOOLED THE WORLD
HEIR TO A DARK INHERITENCE
  (Secret Heirs of Powerful Men)

Maisey Yates

Forged in the Desert Heat

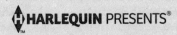
HARLEQUIN PRESENTS®

Recycling programs
for this product may
not exist in your area.

ISBN-13: 978-0-373-13209-6

FORGED IN THE DESERT HEAT

First North American Publication 2014

Copyright © 2014 by Maisey Yates

Printed in U.S.A.

Forged in the Desert Heat

To my daughter. Never be afraid to stand up for yourself, or to stand for what's right. You're the hero of your story.

CHAPTER ONE

SHEIKH ZAFAR NEJEM scanned the encampment, the sun burning what little of his skin was revealed. He was as covered as he could possibly be, both to avoid the harsh elements of the desert, and to avoid being recognized.

Though, for most, the odds of that would be low out here, hundreds of miles from any city. But this was his home. Where he'd been raised. The place where he'd made his name as the most fearsome man in Al Sabah.

And considering his competition for the position, there was weight to the title.

Nothing seemed out of the ordinary here. Cooking fires were smoldering, and he could hear voices in the tents. He stopped for a moment. This was no family encampment, but that of a band of highway men. Thieves. Outlaws, not unlike himself. He knew these men, and they knew him. He had a tentative truce with them, but that didn't mean he was ready to show himself.

It didn't mean he trusted them. He trusted no one.

Especially not now.

Not now that there was certain to be unrest. Anger, backlash over his installation in the palace. On the throne.

Back to his rightful position.

The Gypsy Sheikh's return had not been met with delight, at least not in the more "civilized" corners of the country. His uncle had done far too efficient a job in destroying his reputation for anyone to be pleased at his coronation.

If only he could dispel the rumors surrounding his exile. But he could not.

Because they were true.

But here, among the people who felt like his own—among the people who had suffered most at his uncle's hand—there was happiness here at least. They knew that whatever his sins, he had been working to atone.

Zafar looked out toward the horizon, all flat and barren from this point to Bihar. There was one more place to stop and seek shelter, but it was another five hours' ride, and he didn't relish the idea of more time spent in the saddle today.

He dismounted his horse and patted the animal, dust rising from his black coat. "I think we'll take our chances here," he said, leading him to a makeshift corral, where other horses were hemmed in, and opened the gate.

He closed it, making sure it was secure before walking back toward the main tent.

One of the men was already coming out to greet him.

"Sheikh," he said, inclining his head. "A surprise."

"Is it? You had to know I was heading back to Bihar." A growing suspicion. The desert was vast and it seemed strange to intersect with Jamal's band of thugs at this particular moment.

"I may have heard something about it. But there is more than one road to the capital city."

"So you had no desire for a meeting with me?"

The other man smiled, dark eyes glinting in the golden light. "I didn't say that. We were hoping to run into you. Or, at least, someone of your means."

"My means are still limited. I haven't yet been back to Bihar."

"And yet, you do find ways to acquire what you need."

Zafar looked the man over. "As do you. Will you invite me in?"

"Not yet."

Zafar knew something wasn't right. His truce with Jamal and his men was tentative. It was probably why they wanted to see him. He was in a position to put a stop to what they did out here in the desert, and he knew the places they liked to hit.

They weren't dangerous men; at least, they weren't entirely without conscience. And so they were on the bottom of a long list of concerns, but, as was human nature, they clearly believed themselves more important in his world than they were.

"Then have you gifts to offer me in place of hospitality?" Zafar asked dryly, a reference to common custom out in the desert.

"Hospitality will come," Jamal said. "And while we don't have gifts, we do have some items you might take an interest in."

"The horses in the corral?"

"Most are for sale."

"Camels?"

"Them, as well."

"What use have I for camels? I imagine there is an entire menagerie of them waiting for me in Bihar. Cars, as well." It had been a long time since he'd ridden in a car. Utterly impractical for his lifestyle. They were a near-foreign thought now, as were most other modern conveniences.

The other man smiled, his teeth brilliantly white against his dark beard. "I have something better. An offer we hope might appease you."

"Not a gift, though."

"Items this rare and precious cannot be given away, your highness."

"Perhaps you should allow me to be the judge of that."

Jamal turned and shouted toward the tent and Zafar watched as two men emerged, holding a small, blonde woman between them. She looked up at him, pale eyes wide, red rimmed. She wasn't dirty, neither did she look like she'd been handled too roughly. She wasn't attempting an escape, either, but given their location...there would be no point. She would have nowhere to go.

"You have brought me a woman?"

"A potential bride, perhaps? Or just a plaything."

"When have I ever given the indication that I'm the sort of man who buys women?"

"You seem like the sort of man who would not leave a woman in the middle of the desert."

"And you would?" he asked.

"In no uncertain terms, Your Highness."

"Why should I care about one Western woman? I have a country to consider."

"You will buy her, I think. And for our asking price."

Zafar shrugged and turned away. "Ransom her. I'm sure her loved ones will pay much more than I am willing or able to."

"I would ransom her, but it is not my intention to start a war."

Zafar stopped and turned, his muscles locked tight, his heart pounding hard. "What?"

"A war, Sheikh. It is not in my best interest to start one. I don't want those Shakari bastards all over my desert."

Shakar was the closest neighboring country to Al Sabah and relations between the two nations were at a breaking point, thanks to Zafar's uncle. "What does Shakar have to do with this woman? She's Western, clearly."

"Yes. Clearly. She is also, if we believe her ranting from when we first took her, American heiress Analise Christensen. I imagine you have heard the name. She is betrothed to the Sheikh of Shakar."

Yes, he had heard the name. He was largely cut off from matters of State but he still heard things. He made sure he did. And clearly, Jamal made certain he heard things, as well. "And how is it I play into this? What is it you want with her?" he spat.

"We can start a war here, or end one, the choice is yours. Also, with the wrong words in the right ear, even if you take her, but threaten us? We can put you in a very bad position. How is it you ended up with her? The future bride of a man rumored to be the enemy of Al Sabah? Your hands are bound, Zafar."

In truth, he would never have considered leaving the woman here with them, but what they were suggesting was blackmail, and one problem he didn't need. One problem too many.

So, buy her and drop her off at the nearest airport.

Yes. He could do. He didn't have very much money on him, but he didn't think their aim was to get the highest price off the beauty's head so much as to seek protection. Zafar was, after all, ready to assume the throne, and he knew all of their secrets.

He looked down at the woman who claimed to be an heiress, betrothed to a sheikh. Anger blazed from those eyes, he could see it clearly now. She was not defeated, but she was also smart enough to save her energy. To not waste time fighting here and now.

"You have not harmed her?" he asked, his throat getting tight with disgust at the thought.

"We have not laid a finger on her, beyond binding her to keep her from escaping. Where would her value be, where would our protection be, if she were damaged?"

They were offering him a chance to see her returned as if nothing had happened, he understood. If she were assaulted, it would be clear, and Al Sabah, and by extension the new and much-maligned sheikh, would be blamed.

And war would be imminent.

Either from Shakar or from his own people, were they to learn of what had happened under his "watch."

He made an offer. Every bit of money he had. "I'm not dealing," he said. "That is my only offer."

Jamal looked at him, his expression hard. "Done." He extended his hand, and Zafar didn't for one moment mistake it as an offer for a handshake. He reached into his robes and produced a drawstring coin purse, old-fashioned, not used widely in the culture of the day.

But he'd been disconnected from the culture of the day for fifteen years so that was no surprise.

He poured the coins into his hand. "The woman," he said, extending his arm, fist closed. "The woman first."

One of the men walked her forward, and Zafar took hold of her arm, drawing her tight into his body. She was still, stiff, her eyes straight ahead, not once resting on him.

He then passed the coins to Jamal. "I think I will not be stopping for the night."

"Eager to try her out, Sheikh?"

"Hardly," he said, his lip curling. "As you said, there is no surer way to start a war."

He tightened his hold on her and walked her to the corral. She was quiet, unnaturally so and he wondered if she was in shock. He looked down at her face, expecting to see her eyes looking glassy or confused. Instead, she was looking around, calculating.

"No point, princess," he said in English. "There is nowhere to go out here, but unlike those men, I mean you no harm."

"And I'm supposed to believe you?" she asked.

"For now." He opened the gate and his horse approached. He led him from the enclosure. "Can you get on the horse? Are you hurt?"

"I don't want to get on the horse," she said, her voice monotone.

He let out a long breath and hauled her up into his arms, pulling her, and himself, up onto the horse in one fluid motion, bringing her to rest in front of his body. "Too bad. I paid too much for you to leave you behind."

He tapped his horse and the animal moved to a trot, taking them away from the camp.

"You…you bought me?"

"All things considered I got a very good deal."

"A good…a good deal!"

"I didn't even look at your teeth. For all I know I was taken advantage of." He wasn't in the mood to deal with a hysterical woman. Or a woman in general, no matter her mental state. But he was stuck with one now.

He supposed he should be…sympathetic, or something like that. He no longer knew how.

"You were not," she said, her voice clipped. "Who are you?"

"You do not speak Arabic?"

"Not the particular dialect you were speaking, no. I recognized some but not all."

"The Bedouins out here have their own form of the language. Sometimes larger families have their own variation, though that is less common."

"Thank you for the history lesson. I shall make a note. Who are you?"

"I am Sheikh Zafar Nejem, and I daresay I am your salvation."

"I think I would have been better off if I were left to burn."

Ana clung to the horse as it galloped over the sand, the night air starting to cool, no longer burning her face. This must be what shock felt like. Numb and aware of nothing, except for the heat at her back from the man behind her, and the sound of the horse's hooves on the sand.

He'd stopped talking to her now, the man who claimed to be the Sheikh of Al Sabah, a man whose entire face was obscured by a headdress, save for his obsidian eyes. But before she'd been kidnapped…and it surely had only been a couple of days…Farooq Nejem had been the ruler of the country. A large and looming problem for Shakar, and one that Tariq had been very concerned with.

"Zafar," she said. "Zafar Nejem. I don't know your name. I can't…remember. I thought Farooq…"

"Not anymore," he said, his voice hard, deep, rumbling through him as he spoke.

The horse's gait slowed, and Ana looked around the barren landscape, trying to figure out any reason at all for them to be stopping. There was nothing. Nothing but more sand and more…nothing. It was why she hadn't made an escape attempt before. Going out alone and unprepared in the desert of Al Sabah was as good as signing your own death certificate.

They'd been warned of that so many times by their guide, and after traveling over the desert in the tour group on camelback for a day, she believed him.

So much for a fun, secret jaunt into the desert with her friends before her engagement to Tariq was announced. This was not really fun anymore. And it confirmed what she'd always suspected: that stepping out of line was a recipe for disaster.

She was so fair, too much exposure to the midday sun and she'd go up in a puff of smoke and leave nothing but a little pile of ash behind.

So bolting was out of the question, but the fact that they were stopping made her very, very uneasy. She'd been lucky, so lucky that the men that had kidnapped her had seen value in leaving her untouched. She wasn't totally sure about her new captor.

She took a deep breath and tried to ignore the burn in her lungs, compliments of the arid, late-afternoon air. It was so thin. So dry. Just existing here was an effort. More confirmation on why running was a bad idea.

But she had to be calm. She had to keep control, and if she couldn't have control over the situation, she would have it over herself.

Her captor got down off the horse, quickly, gracefully, and offered his hand. She accepted. Because with the way she was feeling at the moment, she might just slide off the horse and crumble into a heap in the sand. That would be one humiliation too many. She had been purchased today, after all.

"Where are we?" she asked.

"At a stopping point."

"Why? Where? How is it a stopping point?" She looked around for a sign of civilization. A sign of something. Someone.

"It is a stopping point, because I am ready to stop. I have been riding for eight hours."

"Why don't you have a car if you're a sheikh?" she asked, feeling irritated over everything.

"Completely impractical. I live in the middle of the desert. Fuel would become a major issue."

Oh yes. Fuel. Oil. Oil was always the issue. It was something she knew well, having grown up the daughter of the richest oil baron in the United States. Her father had a knack for finding *black gold*. But he was a businessman, and that meant that the search was never done. It was all about getting more. Getting better.

And that was how she'd met Sheikh Tariq. It was how she'd ended up in Shakar, and then, in Al Sabah.

Oil was the grandaddy of this entire mess.

But it would be okay. It would be. She thought of Tariq, his warm dark eyes, his smile. The thought of him always made her stomach flip. Not so much at the moment, but given she was hot, tired, dusty, and currently leaning into the embrace of a stranger, thanks to her klutzy dismount, it seemed understandable.

She straightened and pushed away from him, heart pounding. He was nothing like Tariq. For a start, his eyes were flat black, no laughter. No warmth. But so very compelling…

"Where are we?" she asked, looking away from him, and at their surroundings.

"In the middle of the desert. I would give you coordinates, but I imagine they would mean nothing to you."

"Less than nothing." She squinted, trying to see through the haze of purple, the sun gone completely behind the distant mountains now. "How long until we reach civilization? Until I can contact my father? Or Tariq?"

"Who says I'll allow you to contact them? Perhaps I have purchased you for my harem."

"What happened to you being my salvation?"

"Have you ever lived in a harem?" He lifted a brow. "Perhaps you would like it."

"Do you even have a harem?"

"Sadly," he said, his tone as dry as the sand, "I do not. But I am only just getting started in the position as sheikh, so there is time to amass one."

She nearly choked, fear clutching at her. "I am…stranded in the middle of a foreign desert.…"

"It's not foreign."

"Not to you!" she said.

"Continue."

"I am stranded in the desert with a stranger who claims he's a sheikh, a sheikh who bought me, and you are joking about my future! I have no patience for it."

She had no patience left in her entire body. At this moment, she had two options: get angry, or sink to the ground and cry. And crying was never the preferred option. No, the schools she'd attended, the ones she'd been sent to after her mother left, had been exclusive, private and very strict. She'd been taught that strength and composure were everything. She'd been taught never to run when she could walk. Never to shout when a composed, even statement would do. And she'd learned that tears never helped anything in life. They didn't change things. They hadn't brought her mother back home, certainly.

So she was going with anger.

His manner changed, dark brows locking together. His black eyes glittering with dark fire. He tugged at the bottom portion of the scarf, which had kept most of his face hidden until that moment, and revealed his lips, which were currently curled into a snarl.

"And you think I have the patience for this? These men are playing at starting a war between two nations simply to keep their petty ring of thieves intact. They are trying to buy my loyalty with blackmail. Because they know that if your precious Tariq finds out you were taken by citizens of Al Sabah, or God forbid, they find out the Sheikh of Al Sabah possessed you for any length of time against your will, that the tenuous truce we have between the countries will shatter entirely. How do you suppose my patience is?"

She blinked, feeling dizzy. "I…I'm going to start a war?"

"Not if I play it right."

"I imagine putting me in your harem wouldn't defuse things."

"True enough. But then…perhaps I want the war."

"What?"

"I am undecided on the matter."

"How can you be undecided on the matter?"

"Easily," he said. "I have yet to have a look at any of the papers left behind by my uncle. I have had limited contact with the palace since finding out I was to be installed as ruler."

"Why?"

"Could have something to do with the fact that my first, albeit distant, act was to fire every single person who worked for my uncle. Regime changes are rough."

"Is this a…hostile takeover?"

"No. I am the rightful heir. My uncle is dead."

"I'm sorry." Her manners were apparently bred into her strongly enough that they came out even in the middle of a crisis of this magnitude.

"I'm not. My uncle was the worst thing to happen to Al Sabah in its history. He brought nothing but poverty and violence to my country. And stress between us and neighboring countries." His dark gaze swept over her. "You are unfortunate enough to have become a pawn in the paradigm shift. And I have yet to decide how I will move you."

CHAPTER TWO

FOR ONE MOMENT, Zafar almost felt something akin to sympathy for the pale woman standing in front of him. Almost.

He had no time for emotions like that. More than that, he was nearly certain he had lost the ability to feel them in any deep, meaningful way.

He'd spent nearly half of his life away from society, away from family. He'd had no emotional connections at all in the past fifteen years. He'd had purpose. A drive that transcended feeling, that transcended comfort, hunger, pain. A need to keep watch over Al Sabah, to protect the weakest of his people. To see justice served.

Even at the expense of this woman's happiness.

Fortunately for her, while he imagined she would be delayed longer than she would like, he had a feeling their ultimate goals would be much the same. Seeing her back to Tariq would be the simplest way to keep peace, he was certain. But he had to figure out how to finesse it.

And finesse was something he generally lacked.

Brute force was more his strength.

"I don't like the idea of that at all," she said. "I'm not really inclined to hang around and be moved by you. I want to go home." She choked on the last word, a crack showing in her icy facade. Or maybe the shock was wearing off. It was very likely she'd been in shock for the past few days.

He remembered being in that state. A blissful cushion

against the harsh reality of life. Oh yes, he remembered that well. It had driven him out into the desert and the searing heat had hardly mattered at all.

He hadn't felt it.

He was numb. Bloody memories blunted because there was no way he could process them fully. Deep crimson stains washed pink by the bone-white sun.

If she was lucky, she was being insulated in that way. If not…if not he might have a woman dissolving in front of him soon. And he really didn't have the patience for that.

"I'm afraid that's impossible."

"Right. War. Et cetera."

"You were listening. Now, hold that thought while I go and set up a tent. Can you do that? And can you also not wander off?"

"I don't have a death wish," she said. "I'm not about to wander off into the desert at night. Or during the day. Why do you think I haven't escaped?"

"That begs the question how you were taken in the first place." He took the tent, rolled up and strapped to the back of his horse, and walked over the outcrop of rock. He would hide them from view as best as he could.

Jamal and his men were hardly the only thieves, or the only danger, they could face out in the desert.

"I was on a desert tour. Of the Bedouin camps in Shakar. On the border."

"So my people went into Shakar to take you?"

She nodded. "Yes."

"You are damned lucky they knew who you were." He didn't like to think of the fate she might have met otherwise.

"My ring," she said. "It gave me away. It was part of the Shakari crown jewels." She flexed her fingers, bare now. "They kept that. But then, they would be pretty bad thieves if they didn't."

"Fortunate you had it," he said. "Odd they did not produce it as proof."

Pale eyes widened, panic flaring in their depths. "But you must know about me," she said. "You must know that Tariq planned to marry soon. I would imagine even base intelligence would have brought you that bit of information."

"An alliance that pertains to the political, I believe," he said.

"Yes. And he loves me."

"I'm sure he does," Zafar said dryly.

"He does. I'm not fool enough to think that my connections have nothing to do with it, but we've been...we've been engaged for years. Distantly, but we have spent time together."

"And you love him?"

"Yes," she said, tilting her chin up, blue eyes defiant. "I do. With all my heart. I was looking forward to the marriage."

"When was the marriage to take place?"

"A few months yet. I was to be introduced to his people, our courtship to be played out before the media."

"But your courtship has already taken place."

"Yes. But you know...appearances. I mean, that's the whole point of not taking me straight back to Shakar, isn't it? Appearances. You don't want Tariq to know your people, or by extension, you were involved in this. And you don't want to appear weak. You don't want people to know it happened on your watch." She nodded once, as if agreeing with herself. "That's a big part of it, isn't it?"

"I haven't had a single day in the palace yet. I don't want to be at the center of a scandal involving a kidnapped future sheikha of a neighboring country, so yes, you're right."

"I see."

"What is it you see, *habibti*?" he asked, the endearment flowing off his tongue. It had become a habit to call women that. Because it was easier than remembering names. Safer, in many ways. It kept them at a distance and that was how he preferred it.

Life in the desert, on the move, made it difficult to find lovers, but he had them in a few of his routine stops. A couple of widows in particular Bedouin camps, and a woman in the capital city who was very good at supplying him with necessary information.

She squinted, pale eyes assessing him. "That this is a threat to you personally."

"I am not the most well-liked man in Al Sabah. Let's just say that. This is an issue when one means to rule a country."

It was the understatement of the century. If he had been recognized anywhere in the city while his uncle was in command, his life would have been forfeit. His exile had been under the darkest of circumstances, and since then, he'd hardly done anything to improve his standing, particularly with those loyal to his uncle.

His loyalty was to the Bedouins. To ensure they never suffered because of his uncle's rule, and without him, they would have. No medical, no emergency services of any kind. His uncle had put them at the mercy of foreign aid while taxing them with particular brutality.

They had become Zafar's people.

And now…now somehow he had to assume the throne and unite Al Sabah again, redeem himself in the eyes of the people in the cities while not losing the people in the desert.

And without incurring the wrath of the Sheikh of Shakar.

Not a tall order at all.

"It doesn't really make me feel all that good about being out here with you."

"I'm certain it does not. I'm also certain that's not my problem. Now, I have a tent to pitch so that we don't have to sleep in the open."

"You expect me to sleep in a tent with you?"

"I do. The alternative is for one of us to sleep without any sort of protection and I'm not going to do that. I assume you won't, either. You should see all the bugs that come out at night."

Ana shuddered. The idea of sleeping in the vast openness of the desert with no walls around her at all was completely freaky, and she didn't want any part of it. But the thought of sleeping next to this man…this stranger…was hardly any better.

Her one and constant comfort was the fact that he didn't want to start a war.

Maybe she should tell him she was a virgin. And that Tariq knew it. So if he tried anything he shouldn't there would be no getting out of it. War would be upon him.

A war over her hymen. Yuck. But potentially true.

And if it would help protect her, well, she wasn't above using it as an excuse. But she would save it. Because… yuck.

"How long do you intend to keep me with you?" she asked, watching as he began to work at setting up what looked to be a far-too-small tent.

"Until I no longer need to." He was wearing so many layers, robes to keep him protected from the sun, that it was hard to tell just how his body was shaped, and yet, because of the ease of his movements and the grace in them, she got a sense that he was a man in superior physical condition.

Not that she should notice or care.

"That's not very informative."

"Because I have no more information to give. I will

have to evaluate the situation upon arrival at the palace, and until then, we are stuck with each other."

He continued to work, his movements quick and agile, practiced.

"So…you do this a lot?"

"Nearly every night."

"You buy kidnapped women and then carry them off on your horse every night?"

"I was just referring to the tent."

"I know," she said, looking up at the sky, vast and dotted with stars. "Just trying to lighten the mood." Otherwise she really would cry. She didn't have enough energy for anger anymore. Lame jokes were her last line of defense.

And she couldn't fall apart. Not now. Her father would need her to keep it together, to make sure she made it back to him. Back to Tariq. She'd done everything right, had spent so many years doing her best to be helpful. To not be a burden.

Falling down in the home stretch like this was devastating.

"Technically," he said, tying a knot in a rope at the top of the tent. "I didn't buy you. I ransomed you."

"That does sound nicer."

"Think of it that way then. If it helps."

"A small comfort, all things considered, but I'll take it."

"There, it is done. Are you ready to sleep?"

No and yes. She didn't want to get into the tent with him and sleep on the ground. It was demoralizing. More than that, it was scary. The idea of being so close to him made her heart pound, made her feel dizzy. But she was also ready to collapse with exhaustion. No matter that Zafar was a stranger, he wasn't her kidnapper. He wasn't the same as the men who'd been holding her these past few days.

No matter how austere and frightening he was, he had saved her from her kidnappers.

"Oh…thank you," she said, a tear sliding down her cheek. "Thank you so much."

And something in her broke that she hadn't even realize had been there. The dam on her emotions that had been keeping her strong, keeping her from falling apart since she'd been taken from the camp all those days ago. Or maybe the same dam that had been in place for years, holding back tears for ages, and unable to withstand this new onslaught of life's little horrors.

And control was suddenly no longer an option.

A sob shook her body, emotion tightening her throat. And then she broke down completely. Great gasps of breath escaping, tears rolling down her face.

He didn't move to comfort her; he didn't move at all. He simply let her cry, her sobs echoing in the still night. She didn't need his touch. She just needed this. This release after days of trying to be strong. Of trying not to show how scared and alone she felt.

And when she was done she felt weak, embarrassed and then angry again.

"Done?"

She looked up and saw him regarding her with an expression of total impassivity. Her outburst hadn't moved him. Not at all. Not that she really wanted comfort from this big…beast man. But even so. A little reaction would have been nice. Sympathy. Offer of a cold compress or smelling salts or…something.

"Yes," she said, her throat still tight, her voice croaky. "I am done. Thank you."

"Ready to sleep?"

"Yes." The word escaped on a gust of breath. She was completely ready to collapse where she was standing. She didn't know how that had happened. How exhaustion had taken over so completely.

And then she realized she was shaking. Shivering. She couldn't do this. She had to be strong and keep control. She had to hold it together.

"I don't know why," she said through chattering teeth.

He swore, at least she assumed it was a swearword, based on the tone, and took two long strides toward her, gripping her by the arms and drawing her into the warmth of his body. It wasn't a hug. She knew that right away. This was no show of affection; it was just him trying to keep her from rattling apart.

She trembled violently, his strong arms, his chest, a wall of support. It was amazing that he smelled as good as he did. Yes, it was a weird thought, but it was simple, basic and one she could process.

All those layers in the heat and she would have imagined he might smell like body odor. Instead he smelled spicy, like fine dust and cloves. And he did smell of sweat, but it wasn't offensive in any way. He smelled like a man who had been working, a man who had earned every drop of that sweat through honest effort.

That, somehow, made it seem different than other sweat.

Not that she could really claim to be an expert in the quality of sweat, male or otherwise, but for some reason, that was just how it seemed to her.

This current train of thought was probably a sign of a complete mental breakdown. Highly likely, in fact. Yes, very likely, because she was still shaking.

And adding to the signs of a breakdown, was the fact that part of her wanted to curl her fingers around his robe and hold him tightly to her. Cling to him. Beg him not to let her go.

"The nearest mobile medical unit is…not very near,"

he said, his voice rough. "So please don't do anything stupid like dying."

"If I were dead, how much help would a mobile medical unit be anyway?" she asked, resting her head on his chest, something about the sound of his heartbeat making her feel more connected to the world. To living. She was so completely drained; it felt like it was the reminder of his life that kept her connected with hers. "Besides I don't think I'm dying."

"Does anyone ever think they're dying?"

"I'm not hurt."

"How long has it been since you had a drink?"

She thought back. "A while. I'm not even really sure how many days it's been since I was kidnapped."

"I'm going to put you in the tent."

She nodded, and at the same time found her feet being swept off the ground, as her body was pulled up against his, his arms cradling her, surprisingly gentle for a man with his strength.

He carried her to the tent and set her down on a blanket inside. Then he left her, returning a moment later with a skin filled with water.

"Drink."

She obeyed the command. And discovered she was so thirsty she didn't think she could ever be satisfied.

She pulled the skin away from her lips and a drop ran down her chin. She mourned that drop.

"I hope you weren't saving that," she said.

"I have more. And we'll stop midmorning at an oasis between here and the city."

"Why didn't we stop at the oasis tonight?"

"I'm tired. You're tired."

"I'm fine," she said. His tenderness was threatening to undo her, if you could call the way he was speaking to her now *tenderness*.

"You must be realistic about your own limitations out here," he said. "That is the first and most valuable lesson you can learn. The desert can make you feel strong and free, but it also makes you very conscious of the fact that you are mortal."

She lay down on the blanket and curled her knees into her chest, her back to Zafar. She heard the blanket shift, felt it pull beneath her as he lay down, too.

"The wilderness is endless, and it makes you realize that you are small," he said, his voice deep, accented, melting over her like butter. She felt like the ground was sinking beneath her, like she was falling. "But it also makes you realize how powerful you are. Because if you respect it, if you learn your limitations and work with them, rather than against them, you can live here. You will never master the desert…no man or woman can. But if you learn to respect her, she will allow you to live. And living here, surviving, thriving, that is true power."

Her eyes fluttered closed, and the world upended. "I'm cold," she said, a shiver racking her.

A strong arm came around her waist, and she was pulled into heat, warmth that pushed through to her soul. It was a strange comfort. It shouldn't even be a comfort, and yet it was. Being held by him felt good. Human touch, his touch, soothed parts of her she hadn't known had been burned raw by her nights in the desert.

His fingertip drifted briefly along the line of her bare arm. A soothing gesture. One that stopped the chill. One that made her feel like a small flame had been ignited beneath her skin.

Her last thought before losing consciousness was that she'd never slept with a man's arm around her like this. And the vague sense that she should be saving this for the man she was marrying.

Except that didn't make sense. This was just sleeping.

And she badly needed sleep.

So she moved more tightly into his body and gave in to the need she'd been fighting against ever since she'd been kidnapped.

And slept.

CHAPTER THREE

"You need to wake up now."

Zafar looked down at the sleeping woman, curled up on the floor of the tent like an infant.

The sun was starting to rise over the mountains, and in a moment, the air became heated. Enough that if you breathed too deeply it would scorch your lungs. And he didn't relish riding through the heat of the day. He wanted to get to the oasis, wait it out, then continue on to the city.

He didn't want to spend another night out here with this fragile, shivering creature. He needed to be able to sleep, and he could not sleep beside anyone.

Plus, she was far too delicate. Far too pale. Her skin an impractical shade of pink, her hair so blond it was nearly white, her eyes the same blue as the bleached sky.

She would burn out here in the desert.

She stirred and blinked, looking up at him. "I…" She pushed into a sitting position. "Oh, no. It wasn't a dream."

"No. Sorry. And are you referring to me or the kidnapping? Because I should think I am preferable to a band of thieves."

"The kidnapping in general. This entire experience. Ugh. My whole body hurts. This ground is hard."

"I'm sorry. Perhaps you should talk to the Creator about softening it for you."

"Oh, I see, you think I'm silly. And wimpy and whatever." She pushed a hand through her hair, and he noticed her fingers got hung up in it. He wondered how long it had been since she'd been able to brush her hair. He imagined she hadn't been given the opportunity to bathe or take care of any necessities really.

And he wondered if they had gone with her when she'd had to take care of certain biological needs. If they had stood guard. If they had made her feel humiliated. It heated the blood in his veins. Made him feel hungry for revenge. But he couldn't follow the feeling. Emotion didn't reign in his life. Not now. Emotion lied. Purpose did not.

And it was purpose he had to follow now, no matter the cost.

"I think very little about you, actually. At least, about you as a person. Right now, you are an obstacle. And one that is making me late." He'd been contacted by one of his men. There was an ambassador Rycroft, a crony of his uncle's who was anxious for a meeting. Zafar was about as anxious for it as he was for a snakebite, but he supposed that was his life now.

Meetings. Politics.

"Excuse me?" She stood now, her legs shaky, awkward like a newborn fawn's. "I'm making you late? I didn't ask to be kidnapped. I didn't ask for you to buy me."

"Ransomed. I ransomed you."

"Whatever, I didn't ask you to."

"Be that as it may, here we are. Now get out, I need to take the tent down."

She shot him a deadly glare and walked out of the tent, her chin held high, her expression haughty. She looked like a little sheikha. A pale little sheikha who would likely wither out here in the heat.

"I have jerky in my saddlebags," he said.

"Mmm. Yay for dry salted meat in the heat," she said,

clearly not satisfied to look at him with venom in her eyes. She had to spit it, too.

For all her attitude, she went digging through the bags, and as soon as she found the jerky she was eating it with enthusiasm. "More water?" she asked.

"In the skin."

He continued deconstructing the tent while she drank more water and ate more food. For a woman who was so tiny, she didn't eat delicately.

"Did they feed you?"

"Some," she said, between gulps of water. "Not enough, and I was skeptical of it. So I only ate when I couldn't stop myself."

"Poisoning you, or drugging you would have served no purpose."

"Probably not, but I was feeling paranoid."

"Fair enough."

"But you won't hurt me, will you?" she asked, almost more a statement than a question, pale eyes trained on him.

"You have my word on that."

He would not harm a woman. No matter her sins. Even he had his limits. Though he might see a woman thrown in jail for the rest of her life, but that was an entirely different woman. A different matter.

"I didn't think you would. That's why I slept."

"How many days?"

She shook her head. "I don't know. I was afraid to close my eyes because who knew what might happen. But it only makes things worse. It makes you…think things that aren't real, makes it all blur together and then…it's all scary enough without the added paranoia. I thought I was going crazy."

"Understand this," he said. "I'm not holding you for fun. I am not holding you to harm you in any way. I need to get a better read on the situation. I know this isn't ideal for you, but war during your courtship would be even worse."

"War would be worse in general," she said. "But maybe I can talk to Tariq...."

"Maybe. And maybe it would matter. But there are times when a man must show his strength to protect what is his. There is a time for peace, but when your fiancée has been kidnapped, I am not sure that's the time." He paused. "And then there's how my people will react. It is the sort of thing they expect of me. I will be implicated, make no mistake. Jamal will ensure it. And you know, for many leaders, it wouldn't matter. They could crush the rumors, destroy the rebellion. Me? There is no loyalty to me here. It is not the love of my people chaining me to the throne, but law. If they could see me relieved of the position, many of them would, do not doubt it."

"But you need to rule?"

"I was born to rule. It is my rightful place, stolen from me. I was exiled, banished, and I will not live the rest of my days that way. The throne of Al Sabah is mine now, and I mean to take it."

"Even if you have to hold me to do it?"

"You will be kept in a palace, surrounded by luxury that rivals anything your darling fiancé could produce for you, so I doubt you'll feel to put upon. Consider it a spa retreat."

She looked around them. "Shall I start with sand treatment? Good for the pores, or what?"

"All right, the retreat portion of the vacation starts tonight. For now, consider yourself still on the desert tour. Only this is one-on-one. And you're now with a man who knows the desert better than most people know the layout of the city they grew up in."

"I don't know whether to ask questions about the rocks or the dirt. The beauty is so diverse out here."

"The landscape in Shakar is similar. Perhaps you should

rethink your upcoming marriage if the best you can muster for your surroundings is a bit of bored disdain."

"I'm sorry to have insulted your precious desert. I'm in a bad mood."

"Your mood is the least of my worries, *habibti*. Now—" he put the bundle of tent back onto the horse, took the skin from her hand and refixed it to the saddlebags "—get on the horse, or I shall have to assist you again."

She looked up at the horse and then back at him, genuine distress in her blue eyes. "I can't. I wish I could. But my legs feel like strained spaghetti. It's not happening."

"It's no matter to me. I held you all night. Putting my arms around you again isn't exactly a hardship." Her cheeks turned a brilliant shade of red and it had nothing to do with the sun. He didn't know why he'd felt compelled to tease her that way. He didn't know why he'd felt compelled to tease her at all. He couldn't remember the last time he'd ever felt the least desire to engage in humor or lightness of any kind.

But beneath that was something darker. Something he had to ignore. A pull that he couldn't acknowledge.

"Do what you must," she said, defeated.

He locked his fingers together and lowered his hands, creating a step for her. "Come on," he said.

She looked down and squinted. "Oh, fine." She put one hand on the horse's back and one on his shoulder, placing her foot into his hands and pushing up. He lifted her as she swung her leg over the horse and took her position.

"Front or back, *habibti*, it's no matter to me."

She looked genuinely troubled by the question. And then as though she was calculating which method would bring her into the least contact with his body.

"I...front."

He found the position a bit more taxing, but the alternative was to have her clinging to his back, thighs shaped around his, her breasts pressed to his back. The thought sent a strange tightening through his whole body. His throat down to his stomach, the muscles in his arms, his groin.

No. He had no time for such distraction. She would remain untouched. Protected. He swore it then and there. A vow made before the desert that he would not break.

Fiancée or not, a man who would take advantage of a woman in her position was the basest of creatures.

And are you not more animal than man after your time out here?

No. He knew what was right. And he would see it done.

Right was why he was returning now. Back to a palace that was, in his mind, little more than a gilded tomb. A place that held ghosts. Secrets. Pain so deep he did not like to remember it.

But this had nothing to do with want. Nothing in his life had to do with want; it was simply duty. If doing right meant riding into hell, he would. While the palace wasn't hell, it was close. But there could be no hesitation. No turning back.

And no distractions.

He got on behind her, gripping the reins tightly. "Hold on." He wrapped an arm around her waist. "If we're going to make it back to the palace today, we have to go fast."

Fast was an understatement. They made a brief stop at the oasis, a pocket in a mountain that seemed to rise from the earth, shielding greenery and water from the sun, providing shade and relief from the immeasurable heat.

Sadly, they didn't linger for very long and they were back in the sun, the horse's hoofbeats a repetitive, pounding rhythm that was starting to drive her crazy.

By the time the vague impression of the city, hazy in the distance, came into view, Ana was afraid she was going to fall off the horse. Fatigue had set in, bone deep. She felt coated in a fine layer of dust, her fingers dry and stiff with it.

She needed a bath. And a soft bed. She could worry about everything else later, as long as she had those two things as soon as humanly possible.

This was not her life. Her life was cosseted in terms of physical comforts. A plush mansion, a private all-girls school with antique, spotless furniture and women's college dorms that rivaled any five-star hotel.

Hot baths and soft beds had been taken for granted all of her life. Never again. Never, ever again. She was wretched. She felt more rodent than human at the moment. Like some ground-dwelling creature rooted out of her hole, left to dry out beneath the heat.

As they drew closer she could see skyscrapers. Gray glass and steel, just like any city in the United States. But beyond that was the wall. Tall, made of yellow brick, a testament to the city that once had been—a thousand years ago.

"Welcome to Bihar," he said, his tone grim.

"Are you just going to ride in?"

He tightened his hold on her. "Why the hell not?"

He was a funny contradiction. A man who was able to spout poetry about the desert, soliloquies of great elegance. And yet, when he had to engage in conversation, the elegance was gone. On his own, he was all raw power and certainty, but when he had to interact…well, that was a weakness for sure.

"Seems to me a horse might be out of place."

"In the inner city, yes, but not here on the outskirts. Not on the road to the palace. At least not the road I intend to take."

They forged on, through the walls that kept Bihar separate from the desert. They went past homes, pressed together, stacked four floors high, made from sun-bleached brick. Then on past an open-air market with rows of baskets filled to the brim with flour, nuts and dried fruit. People were milling about everywhere, making way for Zafar without sparing a lingering glance.

She turned and looked up at him. Only his eyes were visible. Dark and fathomless. His face was covered by his headdress. No one would recognize him. It struck her then, how funny it was.

The sheikh riding through on his black war horse, a captive in the saddle with him. And no one would ever know.

They continued on, moving up a narrow cobbled street, past the dense crowds, and through more neighborhoods, the houses starting to spread out then getting sparser. The cobbles turned to dirt, a path that followed the wall of the city, in an olive grove that seemed the stretch on for miles. Then she saw it, a glimmer on the hilltop, stretching across the entire ridge: the palace. Imposing. Massive. Beautiful.

White stone walls and a sapphire roof made it a beacon that she was sure could be seen from most points in the city. Bihar might have thoroughly modern buildings that nearly touched the sky, but the palace seemed to be a part of it. Something ethereal or supernatural. Unreal.

Zafar urged the horse into a canter and the palace rapidly drew closer. When they arrived at the gate, Zafar dismounted, tugging at the fabric that covered his face, revealing strong, handsome features. Unmistakable. No wonder he traveled the way that he did. There was no way he would go unrecognized if he didn't keep his face covered. No way in the world.

He reached into the folds of his robes and pulled out...a cell phone. Ana felt like she'd just been given whiplash. Everything about Zafar seemed part of another era. The man had ridden a freaking black stallion through the city streets, and now he was making a call on a cell phone.

It was incongruous. Her brain rejected it wholly, but it couldn't argue with what she was seeing. Her poor brain. It had tried rejecting this entire experience, but unfortunately, the past week was reality. *This* was reality.

"I'm here. Open the gates."

And the gates did open.

She was still on the horse, clinging to the saddle as Zafar led them into an opulent courtyard. Intricate stone mosaic spiraled in from the walls that partitioned the palace off from the rest of the world, a fountain in the middle, evidence of wealth. As were the green lawns and plants that went beyond the mosaic. Water for the purpose of creating beauty rather than simply survival was an example of extreme luxury in the desert. That much she knew from Tariq.

As if the entire palace wasn't example enough.

She looked at Zafar. His posture was rod straight, black eyes filled with a ferocity that frightened her. There was a rage in him. Spilling from him. And then, suddenly, the walls were back up, and his eyes were blank again.

They were met at the front by men who looked no more civilized than Zafar, a band of huge, marauder-type men. Desert pirates. That's what they made her think of. All of them. Her escort included. One of the men, the largest, even had a curved sword at his waist. Honestly, she was shocked no one had an eye patch.

Fear reverberated through her, an echo along her veins, a shadow of what she'd felt when she was taken from the camp and her friends, but powerful enough that it clung to every part of her. Wouldn't let her go.

She was in his domain. Truly, she had been from the moment she'd been hauled across the border from Shakar to Al Sabah, but here, with evidence of his power all around, it was impossible to deny. Impossible to ignore.

His power, his strength was frightening. And magnetic.

It drew her to him in a way she couldn't fathom. Made her heart beat a little faster. Fear again, that was all. It could be nothing else.

"Sheikh," one of them said, inclining his head. He didn't even spare her a glance.

"Do you need help dismounting?" Zafar asked.

"I think I've got it, thanks." She climbed down off of the horse, stumbling a little bit. So much for preserving her pride. She looked over at Zafar's sketchy crew and smiled.

"We shall need a room prepared for my guest. I assume you saw to the hiring of new servants?"

She nearly laughed. Guest? Was that what she was?

The largest man nodded. "Everything has been taken care of as requested. And Ambassador Rycroft says he will not be put off any longer. He insists you call him as soon as you are in residence."

"Which, I suppose is now," Zafar said, his voice hard, emotionless. "Take the horse."

"Yes, Sheikh."

If any of his men were perturbed by the change in status they didn't show it. But then, she imagined that Zafar had always been the one in charge. That he had always been sheikh to those who followed him.

Questioning him wasn't something anyone would do lightly. He exuded power, strength. Danger. Everything that should have repelled her. But it didn't. It scared her, no mistake, but it also fascinated her. And that scared her on a whole new level.

"Your things?" the other man asked.

"I have none. Neither has she. Remedy that. I want the woman to have a wardrobe of new clothing before the end of the day. Understood?"

The man arched one brow. "Yes, Sheikh."

Oh, good grief. They were going to think she was the starter to his harem. Or at least they would think she was his mistress. But there was no way to correct it now. This was an unprecedented point in Al Sabah's history. Zafar was taking over the throne, and the entire palace clearly had new staff. Zafar would be an completely different sort of leader to the one they'd had before, that much was true.

And it would be such a relief, not just to the people here, but to Tariq's people. She knew that things had been strained between Shakar and Al Sabah, that Tariq had feared war. He'd called her late one night and expressed those fears. She'd valued that. Valued that he cared enough to tell her what was on his mind, his heart.

It was part of why she'd fallen in love with him. Part of why she'd said yes to his engagement offer. Yes, her father had instigated it. And yes, he was a driving force behind it, but she wouldn't have said yes if she wasn't genuinely fond of Tariq.

Fond of him.

That sounded weak sauce. She was more than fond of him. *Love* was the word. No, theirs wasn't a red-hot relationship. But so much of that was to be expected. Tariq was old-fashioned and he'd courted her like an old-fashioned guy. It was respectful.

Plus, he was so handsome. Smooth, dark skin, coal eyes fringed with thick lashes, strong black brows…

She looked back at Zafar and the memory of Tariq and his good looks were knocked completely from her head.

Faced with Zafar, the sharp angles of his face, black beard covering most of his brown skin, obsidian eyes that were more like a dark flame and his lips…she really was quite fascinated by his lips…well, it was hard to think of anything else.

He wasn't smooth. His skin was marked by the sun, by wind. There was nothing refined about him. He was like a man carved straight from the rock.

She wasn't sure *handsome* was the right word for it. It seemed insipid.

"Shall we go in? It is my palace, though I have not been back here in fifteen years. I was born here. Raised here."

Which meant he'd come into the world like everyone else, rather than being carved from stone, so there went that theory.

"Must be…nice to be back?" She watched his face, saw no expression change. If she hadn't caught that moment of intense, dark emotion at the gates, she would think he felt nothing at all. "Strange? Sad?"

"It is necessary that I'm back. That is all."

"I'm sure you feel something about being back."

"I feel nothing in general, Ms. Christensen," he said, addressing her by her name, any part of it, for the first time. "I should hardly start now. I have a country to rule."

"But you're…human," she said, though it sounded more like a question than a statement. "So, I'm sure you feel something."

"Purpose. Every day since my exile there has been one thing that has enticed me to open my eyes each morning, and that has been the belief that my people need me. That it is my duty and my right to lead this country, to care for these people, as they should be led and cared for. Not in the manner my uncle did it. Purpose is what has driven me for nearly half of my life, and purpose is what drives me now. Emotion is unnecessary and weak. Emotion lies. Purpose doesn't."

In so many ways, he echoed a colder, harsher version of what she'd always told herself. That doing right was what mattered. That when people stopped doing right and started serving themselves, things fell apart. Utterly and completely.

She'd seen it in her own family. She'd never wished to bring the kind of destruction her mother had, so she'd set out to be better. To be above selfishness. To do the right thing, the thing that benefitted others before it benefitted her.

To take care, instead of destroy. To be a blessing instead of a burden.

But hearing it from his lips, it seemed…wrong. At least she acknowledged emotion; she just knew there were more important things in life than giddy happiness. Giddy happiness was fleeting, and selfish. She felt it was just her mission to make sure she didn't put her feelings above the happiness of others. There was nothing wrong with that.

"You know what else doesn't lie? My muscles. I'm so stiff I can hardly move."

"A bath then. I will have one drawn for you."

"Th-thank you."

"You sound surprised."

"You're giving me nicer things than my last kidnapper."

"Savior, Analise. I think the word you're looking for is *savior*."

She looked into his midnight eyes and felt something tug, deep and hard inside of her. Something terrifying. Something that touched the edge of the forbidden. "No, I really don't think that's the word I'm looking for."

"Come," he said, walking toward the doors of the palace.

Zafar didn't wait for the double doors to open for him. He pushed against them with both palms, flinging them wide, the sound of the heavy wood hitting the stone walls echoing in the antechamber.

He simply stood for a moment, and waited. For what he did not know. Ghosts, perhaps? There were none. None that were visible, though he could almost feel them. The pain, the anguish this place had witnessed seemed to echo from the walls and he felt it deep down in his bones. If he listened hard enough, he was certain he could still hear his mother screaming. His father crying.

The air was heavy. With memory, with a cold, stale scent that lingered. Probably had more to do with the stone walls than with the past.

He'd spent years living in a tent. Hell, it had been over a year since he'd actually been in a building that wasn't made from canvas. The walls were too heavy. Too thick. Making the air even harder to breathe.

He wanted to turn and run, but Ana was behind him. He felt like an animal being herded into a cage, but he wouldn't show that weakness. He couldn't.

So he took another step inside. Into darkness, into the place that had seen so much death and devastation. It was a step back into his past. One he wasn't prepared to take, but one that had to be taken.

"Zafar?"

He felt a small hand on his arm and he jerked away, looking down at Ana. She didn't shrink back, but he could see something in her wilt. Unsurprising. She must think him more beast than man, but then, there was truth in that.

"We shall have your bath run for you," he said, his voice tight, cold, even to his own ears.

He had no choice but to move forward. To embrace this because it was his destiny. And his penance. He gritted his teeth and walked on.

Yes, this was his penance. He was prepared to pay it now.

CHAPTER FOUR

IT WAS ZAFAR'S great misfortune that Ambassador Rycroft was near and insisted on a meeting immediately. With Zafar in his robes, filthy from traveling. He had no idea how he must appear to the immaculately dressed, clean-shaven man who was sitting in his office now. He had very little idea of how he appeared at all. He didn't make a habit of looking at mirrors.

The man was, per the paperwork he'd seen of his uncle's, important to the running of the country. At least he had been. Zafar suspected that many of the "trade agreements" ran more toward black market deals. But he lacked proof at the moment.

They'd been making tentative conversation for the past few minutes, and Zafar felt very much like a bull tiptoeing through a china shop.

"This regime change has been very upsetting to those of us at the embassy."

"I am sorry for that," Zafar said. "My uncle's death has inconvenienced you. I'm not certain why he couldn't postpone it."

Rycroft simply looked at him, offense evident in his expression. "Yes, well, we are eager to know what you intend to do with the trade agreements."

"Your trade agreements are the least of my concern." Zafar began to pace the room, another move that clearly unnerved his visitor. He supposed he was meant to sit. But he couldn't be bothered. He hated this. Hated having to talk, be diplomatic. He didn't see the point of it. Real men said what they meant; politicians never did. There was no honor in it, and yet, it was how things worked. "I have stepped into a den of corruption and I mean to sort it out. Your trade agreements can wait. Do you understand?"

Rycroft stood, his face turning red. "Sheikh Zafar, I don't think you understand. These trade agreements are essential to the ease of your ascension to rule. Your uncle and I had an understanding, and if you do not carry it out, things might go badly for you."

Anger surged through Zafar, driving his actions before he had conscious thought. All of his energy, seemingly magnified by the feeling of confinement he was experiencing in this place, broke free. He grabbed the other man by the shoulders and pushed him back against the wall, holding him firmly. "Do you mean to threaten me?"

Politicians might use diplomacy. *He* would not.

"No," the ambassador said, his eyes wide. "I would not…I would never."

"See that you do not, for I have erased men from this earth for far less, and don't forget it."

He released his hold on Rycroft and stepped back, crossing his arms over his chest.

"I will go to the press with this," the other man said, straightening his jacket. "I will tell them that they have put an animal on the throne of Al Sabah."

"Good. Tell them," he said, anger driving him now, past the point of reason. Past whatever diplomacy he might have possessed. "Perhaps I will have fewer pale men in suits to deal with if you do."

As she sank down into the recessed tub, made from dazzling precious stone, and the warm water enveloped her sore, dusty body, Ana had to rethink the savior thing.

These bubbles, the oils, the bath salts…it all felt like they, and by extension, Zafar, might very well have saved her life.

She would have liked to stay forever and just indulge, but she knew she couldn't. She didn't just relax and indulge. It wasn't in her. She had to be useful. There was always something to do. Except, right now there wasn't really anything.

Such a strange feeling. She didn't like being aimless. She didn't like feeling out of control. She needed purpose. She needed a project. Something to keep her mind and hands busy. Something to make her feel like she was contributing.

Being kidnapped wasn't engaging much, except the constant war between her fight-or-flight response. It was terrifying, all of it, and yet she didn't know the right thing to do.

She'd been working so hard for so many years. The desert trip was her last and first hurrah. Post-graduation, pre-public engagement. She'd wanted a touch of adventure, but nothing like this.

She pushed up from the bench and stepped out of the bath. There was a plush towel and a robe waiting for her. And she would be lying if she wasn't enjoying it all a little bit. Premature princess points being cashed in now.

Glamorous in theory. And yet, it would be a lot like an extension of the life she already had. Living for appearances. That was all normal to her. She felt like she was always "on." Even with her friends. The elite women's college they'd gone to had encouraged them to be strong, studious and polished. To conform to a particular image. And even when they had personal time, even when they laughed and let the formality drop a bit, that core, that bit of guardedness, still ran through the group just beneath the surface.

She'd always been afraid to show too much of herself.

Those tears in the desert had been some of the most honest emotion she'd let escape in years.

She wrapped herself in the robe and wandered back into the bedroom. "Oh, you are kidding me," she said, looking down at the long, ornate table along the nearest wall. There was a bowl filled with fruit on it. Figs, dates, grapes.

"All I need is a hottie cabana boy with palm fronds standing by to fan me," she muttered, taking a grape from the cluster and popping it into her mouth.

"I see you're finding everything to your liking."

She whipped around and saw Zafar striding through her bedroom doors. He looked…different. He had lost the headdress and heavy traveling robes, in favor of a white linen shirt and a pair of pale dress pants. His long hair was wet, clean and tied back. He had kept the beard, but it was trimmed short.

Somehow, he looked even more dangerous now, with this cloak of civility. Because at least before, he was advertising that he was a hazard. He had danger signs and flares all over him before. This great hairy beast with a full beard and flowing robes. With windburned skin and a thin coating of dirt. And the sweat smell. Not forgetting that.

But now she felt she could see more of him, and it displayed, to her detriment, just how handsome he truly was. Square jawed with a strong chin, and yet again, the lips.

Why was she so fascinated by his lips? Men's lips weren't that big a deal.

"Everything is lovely, all things considered."

"What things considered?"

"Does the phrase 'gilded cage' mean anything to you?"

He shook his head. "No. You are comfortable?"

She let out an exasperated sigh. "Yes. More or less. But I would feel more comfortable if I could let my father or Tariq know I was safe."

"I'm afraid that isn't possible." He started pacing over

the high-gloss obsidian floor. A caged tiger. That was what
he reminded her of. The thought sent a little shiver of fear
chasing down her spine. "I was hardly exaggerating when
I said this incident could push us into war. Neither of us
want that, am I right?"

"They must be frantic!" she said. "Honestly, can you…
can you channel what it might be like to feel, just for a second? They probably think I'm dead. Or sold. Which I was.
But…but they probably think I'm in grave peril. I could
talk to Tariq. At least give me a chance."

He shook his head. "Things are far too tenuous for me
at the moment. Let me tell you a story."

"I hope it has a happy ending."

"It hasn't ended yet. You may well decide how it does
end, so listen carefully. There once was a boy, who grew
up in an opulent palace, fully expecting one day to be
king. Until the castle was invaded by an enemy army, an
enemy army who clearly knew how to get direct access
to the sheikh and sheikha. They were killed. Violently.
Horribly. Only the boy was spared. He would be king; at
sixteen, he could very well have ruled. But there was a
problem. An inquiry, suggested by the boy's uncle, which
indicated he was to blame for the death of his parents. And
he was found guilty."

There was no emotion in Zafar's voice. There was nothing. It was more frightening than if there had been rage,
malice, regret. Blank nothingness when speaking of an
event like that, total detachment when she knew he was
talking about himself…it was wrong. It was frightening,
how divorced from it he was.

It made her wonder if she was as safe with the dynamic
ruler as she'd initially imagined.

"Exiled to the desert for fifteen years under a cloud.
The uncle ruled, the people fell into despair, the country to

near ruin. And who was to blame? The boy, of course. A boy who somehow survived those years alone and is now a man. A man who must now assume the throne. You see what is stacked against me?"

"I understand," she said, shifting, the stone floor cold beneath her bare feet. She suddenly became very conscious that she was wearing a robe with nothing beneath it. "But let me tell you a story about a girl and…and…no, let me just say, I disappeared some six or seven days ago from a desert tour I wasn't supposed to be on. My friends are probably frantic. My fiancé is probably…concerned." Devastated might be a stretch. Tariq was a very even-tempered man. "My father…" She nearly choked then. "My father will be destroyed. I am all that he has…you have to understand."

Even as she said it, she hoped it was true. Strange that she was wishing for her father to be distressed, but…but she was always so afraid that his life was easier without her. It had been for her mother. No child to take care of. No one to break her lovely things.

"And *you* have to understand this. Inquiries are being made about you. Discreet ones, but it is happening. Kazeem received a phone call with a very clear threat. That the future Sheikha of Shakar was missing, and should she be found on Al Sabahan soil my reign will hold a record for brevity."

"Oh," she said, feeling dazed.

"I am all this country has," he said, his voice hard, echoing in the room. "If there is to be a future for my people, I must remain on the throne. There is no room for negotiation."

"So, what if I try to leave?"

"You will be detained. But I seriously doubt you will try to leave."

"Why?"

"Because you're a sensible woman. A woman who wouldn't want blood on her hands." He looked at her, his eyes taking on a strange, distant quality. "Take it from a man who knows, *habibti*. Whether you spill it with your own hand or not, blood won't come clean."

She believed him. Believed it was true. Believed that he knew what it meant to have blood on his hands. Not for one second would she doubt it.

Could she do it? Could she risk it?

The entire thing made her uneasy, but she hardly had a choice. She could try and run, she could try to find her way back on her own, try to call Tariq, who would storm the castle and...and...oh dear.

She looked at Zafar. Did she really trust this man? That he would release her? That he would do what he said?

She did. Because she'd been alone with him in the desert overnight, and he'd slept with his arm curled around her waist to keep her from shivering. Because when she'd needed touch, no matter whether he understood it or felt it or not, he had provided it. He hadn't taken advantage of her, had never once touched her inappropriately or in a way that would harm her.

In short, he treated her exactly like a man in his position should treat her, provided he was telling the truth.

"I require an exit strategy, Sheikh," she said.

"What do you mean?"

"When will you release me? Regardless of what is happening. There has to be a set end date. A sell-by."

"I'm not certain I can give you that."

"I require it," she said. "No more than thirty days."

"It shall be done." His agreement, the heavy tone in his voice, did nothing to ease her concerns. Thirty days. Thirty days in this palace, a captive of this man. But with that thought the oddest burst of lightness came through.

More of this solitude. These moments of utter indulgence that weren't for anyone but her.

"I am not holding you prisoner," he said.

"Oh really. So, I'm free to go?" The lightness faded, because the fact remained, she was, essentially, Zafar's prisoner.

"No," he said, crossing broad arms over his chest. "Under no circumstances."

"Then how am I not a prisoner?"

"Have I tossed you in the dungeon? Is that bread and water on your table there? No. I gave you a bed. Fruit."

"So, I'm a well-fed prisoner with a down pillow."

"If you like. The difference between this and *prisoner* is in many ways the same as the difference between…purchased and ransomed. Whatever makes you feel better."

"A nap, I think."

"Excellent. A nap. And then you will join me for dinner."

"What? Why?"

"Because, *habibti*, I can hardly have you staying here at the palace looking like a prisoner, now can I?"

"Why not? Goes with the fearsome desert-man thing you're rocking."

"A compliment?"

"Not really. Why not?" She reiterated her earlier question.

"Because, it simply won't do. A little investigation on your part and you could find out a lot of very terrible things about me. Most of them very true. And the last thing I need is any suspicion that I am keeping an American woman here against her will."

"Harem rumors shall abound."

He arched a dark brow. "Indeed."

"So what do you want them to think? Because, all

things considered, later, I will be recognized, so I can't be here as…well…a girlfriend."

He laughed, a strange, rusty sound. Clearly not an expression of emotion he'd used in a while. "I do not have girlfriends, Analise."

"Ana," she said. "No one calls me Analise."

"Ana," he amended, "I have lovers, if you can even call them that. Bed partners. Mistresses. Women who satisfy me physically as I satisfy them." His words, dark, rough and uncivilized, like the man himself, should have appalled her. Just as the man himself should have appalled her. But he didn't. And they didn't. Instead they brought to mind lush scenes of him, more golden-brown skin on display than was decent, his arms wrapped around a woman. A rather pale woman with blond hair. She blinked rapidly and tried to dispel the image.

Zafar continued. "I do not have girlfriends. That brings to mind flowers and chocolates. Trips to the cinema. I haven't been to a cinema in…ever. And I have not even seen a movie in at least fifteen years."

A movie theater was a much-less-challenging image. "That's…that doesn't seem possible."

Zafar was a magnified, twisted version of her in some ways. Never taking the time to do normal things because he was so burdened with purpose.

But really, never going to a movie theater? Not seeing a movie in fifteen years? He wouldn't get half of her jokes. But then, she wondered if Tariq watched movies. They'd never talked about that. They'd talked about weighty things like duty and honor and oil.

But not movies. And she actually liked movies.

"I was a bit consumed with daily survival and making sure the Bedouin tribes weren't completely marginalized, but yes, perhaps I should have made more time for taking in films."

"Oh…like you've never had any downtime. You *do* have mistresses," she said, feeling her face get hot. Because those same images were back. And the woman in the vision was a lot clearer this time. And *oh my*. There was no way she should be entertaining that thought. She was too practical to have vivid sexual fantasies.

"Yes, indeed, but I find sex much more interesting than watching television."

Her mouth dropped open, and she really wished she hadn't let it, but she hadn't known it was going to drop open until it did. She closed it slowly. "Well, all right. There's something I'd like to do in bed right about now. Have a nap. So…goodbye."

He inclined his head. "Until dinner. A dress will be sent."

"Good, I was worried. I would hate to look less than my best for you."

He laughed again, that same uneasy, clearly not oft-used sound. "That would be a tragic occurrence."

"Yeah. I know, right? Now out."

"You give an awful lot of orders for a…"

She crossed her arms. "Yes, that's a question…what am I?"

He regarded her closely, his dark eyes searching. "Well, you do have a lot of opinions on how I ought to do things. And you are certainly trained in the art of being royal… when you aren't letting your tongue run away with you."

"You can see my royalty training coming through?" she asked, only half joking.

"Yes. It is in the way you stand, the way you sit. Your composure, even in a difficult situation. And considering I have just had a meeting with an ambassador that has gone very poorly…"

"Have you?"

"I might have threatened to erase him from the earth."

"Oh, dear," she said.

"And he may have threatened to go to the press."

"Indeed."

"Yes, indeed. So it will come as no surprise to anyone that I am in need of a bit of help. Especially since I am due to make a showing in public very soon."

She eyed him critically. "Oh."

"And I gather you're starting to see the problem. And I think you can help me."

She swallowed. She didn't like the sound of this. A slow smile spread across his face, and that made her even more nervous.

"Ms. Christensen, I believe you are here to teach me to be civilized."

Ana had to wonder what the hell he was talking about while she put on her dress, and still while she wandered down the hall.

The palace was on bare-bones staff and eerily quiet. Not like the times she'd stayed at Tariq's palace in Shakar.

There, the palace was constant motion and sound—people moving everywhere, administrative staff, cleaning staff, serving staff, tours often being given in portions of the palace. There was always activity.

Things seemed dead here. Frozen in time. It reminded her of a fairy-tale castle, where all the inhabitants were sleeping. Or maybe turned into furniture and small appliances by a wicked enchantress.

Or maybe just that a new leader had been installed who had no subjects loyal to him beyond the broad expanse of the desert.

That was more likely.

She walked through the empty corridors and she had a sudden thought. A phone. What if she could find a phone?

She hurried through the hall, looking in opened rooms

and in nooks. And there, she found one. An old-fashioned, gilded, rotary phone sitting on a pedestal. Just waiting. She walked over to the table and stood in front of it, her palms sweaty.

She could call Tariq. She knew his personal number by heart. Not because she'd used it so much, but because she'd felt a woman ought to know her fiancé's phone number.

She stood there and imagined what she would say. And what his response would be. What if he mobilized the helicopters? And ground troops. And they swarmed the castle. And everything Zafar was working toward would be utterly destroyed because she'd had to take action.

And worse—a small voice inside of her had to say it— what if he did nothing? What if he waited? What if he too just sat back and did the thing that was most politically expedient?

That thought made her ill. And as much as she'd like to forget she'd ever had it, it was impossible to do. It was insidious, a small worm of doubt that had been burrowing its way into her for days and days now.

What if he didn't care? Sure, threats had been made. Contact established with Zafar on the matter, but this was all so political in nature. What if, when she was now more inconvenient than convenient, Tariq wouldn't really want her at all?

She backed away from the phone, her heart pounding hard. Later. She knew where the phone was now, and if she needed to make a call, she could do it later .

She wandered down a corridor, trying to ignore the sick feeling in her stomach, trying to stop her hands from shaking. She wandered until she heard movement. The kitchen. She could hear dishes and water. Voices. Finally things felt a little less haunted. And from there, she found the dining room. A serving girl was there, pouring a glass of something for Zafar, who was sitting on the floor on pillows in a semi-reclined position, a low table in front of him.

His shoes were off, no regard given to posture or manners. He had, in fact, started eating without her. He was using his hands, as was the custom, and yet somehow it just looked…shocking when he did it. Wholly sensual. He was eating too fast, like a man who had been without food for too long.

She thought of the jerky in his saddlebags. He had at least been without good food for too long.

He scooped a bit of rice in his hand and ate it, then licked his fingers. She felt a sharp, hard tug low in her stomach, one she couldn't pretend she hadn't felt. No matter how much she wished she could.

Dear heaven, if a fine was charged for looking completely disreputable, he would be forced to sell the castle to pay his debt. He just looked…dangerous and wicked, and for some reason none of it was unappealing. None of it at all. His poor table manners, the fact he was eating without her, should have offended and blotted out all the…the dark magnetism she was feeling.

But it wasn't. Why oh why wasn't it?

"Ana," he said, smiling, for the benefit of the serving girl she imagined, because she'd never seen him smile before. He still looked both wicked and dangerous. "Please come in and sit down."

She obliged, positioning herself across from him on a long, cream-colored cushion.

"Dalia, I will need privacy with Ms. Smith for the meal. We have terms to discuss. A business arrangement."

Dalia inclined her head and set the pitcher on the table. "I'll leave this for you, Sheikh. I wouldn't want you to be thirsty." She gave him a look that could only be described as adoring.

"Thank you." He took a long gulp of his drink and waved her away. She went quickly, her head bent down.

"Firstly," Ana said, when they were alone in the cavernous room, "Smith? Ms. Smith?"

"Ana Smith, much less damning than calling you by Analise Christensen, don't you think? No doubt your name will be appearing in the media, if it hasn't already. Though, I have heard nothing so I would venture to say your sheikh is conducting a covert search for you. Even more dangerous in many ways, because I have no way of knowing where he's looking."

"You mean he hasn't mobilized the military and the press and the…Coast Guard?"

"Not that I have seen, no."

"Oh." She knew there was probably a reason, and it wasn't that he didn't care, just that it was strategy. Like the strategy Zafar was employing. Greater good and all. She was just one girl. She wasn't worth uprooting national security over or anything. And stuff.

"You will be kept here at the palace. Public events would be too risky. Really, any showing in public would be. You will be known as Ana or Ms. Smith, as previously stated, and you are here to teach me…manners."

She looked at him, half-civilized and seemingly unconcerned with it. "Manners?"

"That is oversimplifying, perhaps, but that is one thing you will help me with. I am a man too long out of society, and now I must come in as a king people can stand with. They will not stand with a barbarian."

"But your serving girl…Dalia, she seemed to be a fan."

"Dalia is from one of the desert tribes. Her family owes me a debt of gratitude, and she came to serve in the palace until I could secure loyal staff."

"She likes you," she said.

"She's young. She'll get over it."

"You aren't interested?"

"Sweet young virgins are fine for some, but not for me. I don't have any interest in seducing women and breaking hearts. It's not how I am."

Sweet young virgins.

Well, indeed.

"Good. I feel better knowing she's safe." *And knowing I'm safe.*

Like she'd ever really had anything to be worried about. He wasn't a going to force himself on her, that much was obvious.

Yeah, but the seducing was worrisome....

No. Nope. No. She wasn't worried about him seducing her. That implied that she was seducible, and she was not. She so was not. But she was a sweet, kind of young…relatively. Virgin—yeah, she was that for sure—so he wasn't going to be interested. But even if he was it wouldn't matter.

Good grief, Ana, you have lost your fool mind.

He was holding her against her will, kind of, and making her play the part of Miss Manners. She had no reason to feel fluttery about him, and yet she did. Because it was easy to remember what it had felt like to fall asleep with his arm around her. How the weight of it had been warm, his body solid and comforting behind her.

How she hadn't disliked it at all, but had actually wanted to stay there in his embrace. And when she'd woken and he was standing above her, rather than lying with her, she'd been confused. She'd missed his presence.

Because she'd been half-asleep and confused, but still. It was inexcusable.

Feelings like that were a betrayal. A betrayal of the man who had…probably mobilized special forces…quietly…to find her.

In the cold light of day, she feared Zafar. His power over

her, the fact that she didn't have the control. She didn't miss having him sleep next to her. So there.

"What is it you expect me to do? Aside from telling you not to threaten dignitaries with bodily harm" she said. "Teach you which fork you eat your salad with?"

"Maybe," he said, and for the first time she developed a hint of something genuine beneath his hard tone. "Maybe you could teach me how to have meaningful diplomatic interaction. Or at least teach me how to avoid scaring people. Something I failed at today, although, I think he very likely deserved it."

"Wait…are you…serious? You mean you really want me to give you royal lessons?"

"You've passed yours so proficiently. And it would be a way to while away the time. I am officially being crowned in less than a month, and look at me," he said, sweeping a hand over his reclining figure. A fine figure it was, too. And she did look. For a little longer than she probably should have. "I am not the man that these people would want to have lead them."

"Why not? You're…strong and you are able to ransom damsels in distress when the situation calls for it, so… leadership qualities in my opinion."

"And yet, I lack charm, you must admit."

"Yeah, okay, you lack charm a little bit."

"And that cannot be."

"Just…be friendlier."

"I don't know how," he said, the words scraping his throat on the way out. "I spent…countless days in the desert alone. Speaking to no one. Sometimes I traveled with men, but then I had to be a leader, and out there…out there manners don't get things done. Diplomacy is not gutting someone when they make a mistake. I have spent the majority of the past fifteen years alone. And while my horse makes for decent company he does not talk back, which means my skills are limited."

"What is your horse's name? You never said."

Zafar's dark brows locked together. "He doesn't have one."

"How can he not have one?"

"He is the only horse. And besides that, it isn't as though he's likely to get mixed up with other horses, or that it would be unclear as to who his rider is. I travel mostly alone, remember?"

"It's just…I name my pets."

"My horse," he bit out, "is not a pet. Do you name your cars?"

"No. But I mean…people do. Some men even name their…" She trailed off, her cheeks lighting on fire. Why had she said that? What had possessed her? She didn't say things like that in front of men, or in front of trustees for charities she worked with. She knew when to keep quiet. Yeah, she got giggly with her friends, specifically the girls she'd gone on the desert tour with. They would talk about their boyfriends and their various and sundry names for their manparts, in a kind of superior way that always made Ana feel gauche. But she would laugh and blush, and generally play the part of group virgin, since that's what she was.

But she didn't just bust out the innuendo at random.

"I do not," he said, no hint of humor in his face.

"I figured as much. Unnamed horses aside—" in that moment she decided she would name the poor thing "—you really do want my help?"

"I more than want it, I need it. I need to be seen as a man and not an animal. I need to be…a king in the eyes of my people, and if I go on like I did today, it will not happen. All things considered, you might find it in you to ransom me?" he asked.

She breathed the words before she had a chance to think them through. It was a job. A project. A purpose. And she always said yes to a project. "Of course."

CHAPTER FIVE

ZAFAR WASN'T CERTAIN what had possessed him to be so honest. Except, why not? She would not be staying here; in fact, she would never speak of her being here at all. He would forbid it, and she would doubtless see the reasoning. It was all to protect his people, and her future people, after all.

Ana Christensen did not need to see him as an infallible leader, or as a fearsome warrior. Ana Christensen only needed to see him as a man, and see how she might help that man assume the throne with more ease. And preferably without being deposed by the neighboring country.

His gut kicked in at the thought of her seeing him as a man. He gritted his teeth. He did not mean it that way. He tightened the tape around his fists and repositioned himself in front of the bag he'd been pounding on only a moment earlier.

Being in the palace like this, being indoors, made him feel restless. Like he had too much energy and nowhere to channel it. That meant a lot of hours spent swimming laps in the pool, lifting weights or hitting a punching bag.

Anything that kept him from feeling like he had during his meeting with Rycroft. Like violence was a living beast just beneath the surface of his skin, waiting to tear its way out.

Anything to keep him from feeling like he was suffocating behind the walls. Or buried alive in a tomb. A tomb that held the spirits of those lives taken here.

He had spent the years since his exile in the desert. In the open. And he had not been back to the palace since he'd been driven out.

Those two made for a poor combination and created a sensation of claustrophobia he didn't like.

Fortunately, he had little time to worry about it. In a few short weeks he would become the face of the nation, and that meant he had to figure out just what face he would show the world.

Not his real one, naturally. No one wanted to engage in diplomatic discussion with a hollow, emotionless stone. A man who had left weakness and feeling behind him so many years ago he couldn't remember what it had felt like to have them inhabit his body.

Neither did he want to.

He just needed an appropriate mask. And Ana would help him fashion it.

"Kazeem told me that you were… Oh!"

He turned and saw Ana standing in the door to his workout room, her jaw slack, her blue eyes wide. Her eyes, he realized, were most definitely not on his face, but on his sweat-slicked torso. And he would be lying if he denied getting any pleasure from it.

But he would not touch her. Ever. It was impossible. A little lust was hardly worth the security of an entire nation.

And you've followed your cock down that path before, haven't you?

He banished that insidious voice. The one that would see him curled up on the floor crying like a child rather than taking action. He had no room for regret. He could only move forward.

He could not erase his past mistakes. They would always stain. The ghosts would always haunt these halls.

The best he could do was attempt to make the future better. For his people. People who had suffered for far too long at the hands of his uncle. Indirectly, his own hands.

Or perhaps not so indirectly.

"That I was what?" he asked.

"Here. But he didn't mention you were busy."

"You thought I was in here reclining, perhaps?"

"No. But…maybe fencing or something. Not…boxing…with yourself."

"This is how I keep fit. I hang the bag inside my tent when I travel."

"That tiny thing?"

"The bag or the tent?"

"The tent. The bag isn't tiny."

"The tent I had the night I acquired you is not the one I normally travel with." He turned and wiped the sweat from his forehead, then started unwinding the tape that was around his fists.

"Well, to what did I owe the pleasure of the mini-tent experience?" Her perfect, pale cheeks darkened, a pink stain spreading over them. And that blush, the acknowledgment that there was something in that night that might make her blush, threw his mind right back there.

To what it had felt like to have her in his arms. Soft. Petite.

Sweet.

So not for him. Not under any circumstances. Not even if she were just a woman he met on a city street. Even then, she wouldn't be for him. All he could ever do with a flower was bruise the petals.

A flower would wither and die out in the desert. And he wasn't just from the desert; the desert was in him. And his touch would only burn her.

A good thing, then, that she was not just a woman on the street. A fortunate thing that she was off-limits for a million reasons, because if the only reason were her well-being… Well, he simply wasn't that good a man.

But with the fate of a nation resting on whether or not he kept it in his pants? He could keep them zipped.

"I saw no point in carrying the extra weight. I traded with a man I met on the road. A smaller tent, food. And it's fortunate for you I was able to trade or I might not have had the money to buy you."

"Ransom."

"If you like."

She frowned. "I thought we agreed it was a lot less demeaning."

"It makes no difference to me."

"One makes you the hero…the other makes you a bastard."

"You say that like you think I might have a preference between the two."

"I…don't you?"

He lifted a shoulder. "Not particularly. I don't have to be good, Ana, I just have to win. In the end, Al Sabah has to win. The rest…the rest doesn't matter."

"And you'll do anything to win?"

"Anything," he said.

Ana believed him. There was no doubt. The way he said it, so dark and sure and certain, sent a shiver through her body, down into her bones. And yet it didn't repel her. It didn't make her want to run. Perversely, it almost made her want to get closer.

The shock of fear that ran through her body was electric. It sent ripples of warning through her body, showers of sparks that sent crackling heat along her veins.

She felt like a child standing before a fire. Fascinated and awed by the warmth, knowing there was something that might make it all dangerous, but not having any real concept of the damage it could do.

Even having that moment of clarity, she didn't draw back. She did take a step toward him, though. Zafar, in all his shirtless glory.

She'd thought him arresting in his robes. Handsome in the linen tunic, moisture clinging to him from his shower. Without a shirt, his long hair escaping the bonds of the leather strap that normally kept it bound, his body glistening with sweat, a bead of it rolling down his chest, down his abs, sliding along the contours of his hardened muscles…well, just now he defied reality.

He was unlike any man she'd ever seen. All hard, harsh, assaulting masculinity. There was nothing soft about him, nothing to put her at ease or make her feel safe. He bound her breath up in her body, kept it from escaping. Made a rush of feeling whisper over her skin that she couldn't identify or deny.

She knew attraction. She was attracted to Tariq. He was handsome; he gave her butterflies in her stomach. He was a great kisser, though, admittedly at his own insistence their kisses had been brief.

He was everything she could have asked for.

And yet suddenly it seemed like her eyes had just opened and she'd realized there was something more. Something more to men. To the way looking at a man could make her feel. And she wasn't sure what the feeling was exactly. Attraction or something else, because it wasn't attraction like she would have named it last week. Or even two days ago.

But it was something. Something deep and visceral and completely disturbing. And it was holding hands, tightly, perversely, with fear. Perhaps that was why it seemed so intense? Adrenaline combined with attraction, the kind any woman would feel toward a man with such…testosterone-laden qualities. It was like a biological imperative. Strong man, producer of much sperm and good offspring. It was basic high school science, was what it was.

She shook off that line of thinking and tried to focus on the conversation.

"The end justifies the means?" she asked.

"Yes. But the thing you have to understand is that I have a country to run and I must look acceptable while restoring order."

"Please tell me you aren't a crazy dictator, because I don't want to help install a man who's going to turn this country into a military state."

"I won't be any kind of ruler if I can't get my people to accept me. A head is of no use without the body behind it. In two weeks time there is a reception planned, a party celebrating the new sheikh, a show of power for the rest of the world. All brought about by my adviser."

"One of the big dusty, sand-pirate-looking guys?"

She thought he nearly smiled. "Yes."

"And what do they know about that sort of thing?"

"A lot. Before he lost his family Rahm was the leader of the largest tribe in Al Sabah. But after…he couldn't continue on. Needless to say, he is a man who understands power and how to obtain and maintain it."

"He lost his family?"

Zafar swallowed hard. "Yes. Do you know what my uncle did in his time as ruler?"

She looked away from him. "My Al Sabahan history is rusty."

"He raised taxes, most especially on the Bedouins. And trust me when I say it was collected. Even if it had to be taken from their herds. From their tents. Skins and other wares. He took it. He cut services. Mobile medical units, schools. People lost their lives because of the neglect, the poverty."

"Rahm…"

"He suffered, as well. And unlike me...Farooq did have a harem. And when possible...he stole their daughters and brought them here. Unlike me...my uncle did like sweet innocent virgins." His voice was rough, his manner filled with disgust. The rage radiating from him spoke volumes about what manner of man he really was. That at his core, no matter what he said, no matter what he claimed about the end justifying the means, he was a good man. A man who despised hurting the weak. A man who sought justice, no matter the cost.

"Did you save Dalia from that fate?" she asked, her voice choked. She was starting to understand. Zafar had a collection of the broken in his country, surrounding him tightly, acting as his helpers, his staff. And in doing that, he was holding them together.

"Yes," he said. "Thankfully. She is one I was able to help before he managed to take her too far."

"How?"

His expression turned cold. "The men who captured her did not walk away. Let us leave it at that."

She nodded slowly. "Okay."

"I told you, *habibti*," he said, "I have blood on my hands. I will fight for my people. To the death. To the end. But in order to do that...they have to trust me, and while I am confident in my ability to frighten enemies, to seek out justice and destruction for those who would seek to hurt us...I am not confident in my ability as a speaker. Or a diplomat. The guest at a nice dinner."

"If we play things right, maybe I can help you, and you can repair relations between Al Sabah and Shakar. We could have dinner together after Tariq and I marry."

"There. Vision for the future."

"Yes." Except it would be awkward. And terrible, really. Could she ever tell Tariq about this? Would they have to start their marriage out with a lie?

She just didn't like any of it.

There was always the phone. She could always call.

She looked up at Zafar, at his eyes, and she knew she couldn't yet. Not just yet.

She couldn't just leave him. She couldn't just leave him and his people the way things were. He had ransomed her. He could have left her. He could have used her. But he wasn't that man. He was the man who saved girls from being kidnapped. The man who had blood on his hands from saving those who couldn't save themselves.

And that was when she knew she would do it. She could do this. And she wouldn't feel so useless. So at loose ends. If she was going to stay here, then she would accomplish something.

And civilizing Zafar would be no small accomplishment.

"So, do you have a…plan for how you want this to go?"

"I had thought that you might…give me tips?"

"Well, you can't go to a royal dinner wearing only pants."

He laughed, and she felt it all through her body. "Probably true."

"How long has it been since you had a Western-style dinner? At a tall table? And really with a salad fork?"

"A long time."

"Of course, when you entertain here, then it will be up to those visiting you to observe your customs."

"You truly are royally trained." He leaned back against the wall, his shoulders flexing, abs shifting. The man didn't have an ounce of spare flesh on his body.

"It didn't start with Tariq. My mother left when I was really small. And it was just me and my father. My father is a very important businessman. Oil tycoon, actually."

"Ah, and your connection to Tariq and Shakar begins to make sense."

Her face heated. She didn't like the implication. That it was all oil. She knew it was mostly oil, but there were feelings. There were. The fact that she was important on more than one level strengthened things, but it was more than that.

"Anyway, as I got older I used to help him coordinate dinners. Parties. I was hostess a lot of the time. It was hard for him to be a single dad, and he was as involved as he could be with me, and it was…it was nice to be able to help him that way. So you could say that hostessing is one of my talents. As is diplomacy. I went to the kinds of schools people think of as 'finishing schools,' but it's so much more than that. It's a very real education along with intense training for dealing with social situations. I'm versed in handling all kinds of scenarios. Any time you mix a lot of people, some of them competing for jobs or oil rights or money of any kind, things can be tense."

"I assume you have tricks for defusing those situations."

"The art of conversation. Or, more to the point, the art of bland inoffensive conversation. In your case, you'll be dealing with politicians of all different world views, and that will be…"

"A nest of vipers."

"Something like that."

She was starting to feel a little energized now. Starting to feel a renewed sense of purpose. This was giving her something to focus on. A plan, a goal. She liked feeling like she was being useful. Like she was accomplishing things.

This suddenly felt bigger than she was. Fixing a country, changing the shape of things for people. Making a positive impact. Zafar was going to make things better. Zafar wouldn't let the Bedouin people's daughters be taken from their homes to serve some sadistic ruler's fantasies.

And she could be a part of that new beginning. But not if she called Tariq. Not if she let fear push her into running.

No, she wasn't going to run.

She could do this. She might not ever claim credit, but she could start her role as Sheikha of Shakar by doing something valuable.

She trusted Zafar. The realization was a slightly shocking one, but it was the truth. She might not like it an overabundant amount, but she trusted the core of his character. And that was what counted.

"Breakfast in the courtyard tomorrow," she said, because she was sure someone could arrange it. "We'll talk silverware."

"I haven't had very much in the way of real conversation in the past fifteen years, and you want to talk silverware?"

"I told you, the art to getting along with people is bland conversation. How much more bland could it get?"

It turned out that nothing with Zafar could feel bland. Especially not since she was sitting with him in a garden that rivaled anything she'd ever seen. Lush green plants and shocking orange blossoms punctuated by dots of pink covered every inch of the wall that protected the palace from the rest of the world.

The combination of the thick stone wall, the fountains and the shade made the little alcove comfortable, even at midmorning. She had a feeling that by afternoon it would be nearly as unbearable as most other places in Al Sabah, but for now, it was downright pleasant.

"I ordered you an American breakfast," she said, putting her napkin in her lap and folding her hands over it. "Bacon and eggs."

"Do you think that many politicians will be eating bacon and eggs?"

"Fact of life, Zafar, everyone likes bacon. Turkey bacon, by the way, in case you have any dietary restrictions."

"I am not so devout," he said.

It didn't really surprise her. Zafar seemed to depend only on himself. Though, there were people here in the palace. People who had loyalty to him. People he seemed to care for in a strange way.

"It has made the paper," he said.

"What?"

"That I threatened Ambassador Rycroft. He said he saw me in person, and that I am clearly a wild man. That when you look in my eyes you see something barely more advanced than a beast. Of course the press was giddy with his description as they would so love to crucify me."

"I'm sorry."

"This means that my presentation is more important. That this project we are conducting is all the more important."

She nodded slowly. "I understand."

"I have spent too many years alone," he said, his voice rough.

"The men that are here," she said, picking up her fork, "how often did you travel with them?"

"Once a month we might patrol together, but many of them had home bases, while I felt the need to keep moving. To keep an eye on things."

"You said you didn't make a lot of conversation?"

"We didn't. We traveled together, did our best to right the wrongs my uncle was visiting on the desert people. Some of them were men, and the children of men cast out of the palace when my uncle took control. Others, Bedouins who suffered at the hand of the new regime. We didn't get involved in deep talks."

"Why is that?"

"Someone had to keep watch. And I was always happy

to let my men rest. Though we did spend time telling stories."

"Stories?"

"Morality tales, of one sort or another. A tradition in our culture. A truth wrapped in a tale."

She'd heard him do that. Weave reality into a story. Blanketing it so it was more comfortable to hear.

"So you were an army unto yourselves? Out there in the desert?"

"Nothing half so romantic. We were burdened with the need to protect because our people were under siege. It was all born of necessity. Of loss."

"If your people had any idea of what you'd done for them…they would embrace you as their ruler. I know they would."

"Perhaps. Or perhaps what happened in a desert out beyond the borders of the city will make no difference. Perhaps they will only remember what happened here."

"What happened here?"

Zafar gritted his teeth. He hated to speak of it. Of the day his parents died. The day he and his people lost everything.

He hated even more to speak of his role in it, but he didn't have a lot of other options. She had to understand.

She had to know why he was so despised.

"Things had been tense. There were rumors that the royal family might be the target of an attack. And routines were changed, security measures were taken. The sheikh and his wife were preparing to go into hiding until the threat had passed. But there was a breach in the security. And the time that the royal family was to leave the palace was given to their enemies. They never had a chance at escaping. What was meant to be a wholly secure operation, moving them until the threat was over, became the end."

"And how did you get the blame for this, Zafar? I don't understand."

"It was my fault," he said. "And I have spent every year, every day since then, fighting to atone for the destruction I brought on my own people. This is why the papers, why the people, are so anticipating my downfall. My exile was very much deserved. I was responsible for the death of my mother and father, the sheikh and sheikha. And the people of Al Sabah have long memories. They won't forget who they would rather have on the throne. And they won't forget why their most beloved rulers aren't with us any longer. And it's because of me."

CHAPTER SIX

ZAFAR COULD SEE the dawning horror in her eyes, and he was almost glad of it. Because they needed something to break this strange band of tension that was stretching between them, pulling them closer to each other, even as they tried to resist.

Even as he tried to resist. With everything he had in him.

But there was something so very fascinating about her. Something so tempting. But he knew what would happen if he touched her. War aside.

It would be like pouring water on the cracked desert earth. He would take everything she had, soak it in for himself, and at the end of the day, the ground on his soul would still be dry.

"You couldn't have done anything on purpose, Zafar."

"No," he said, his voice harsher than he intended. "I didn't do it on purpose, and in many ways that makes it much worse. I was a fool, manipulated into giving the truth because of trust. Because of love."

She blinked slowly a few times, a look of confusion on her face, as if the idea of him being in love, the whole concept, seemed foreign and unbelievable to her.

Reassuring. That he didn't in any way resemble the soft, stupid boy he'd been. Years in the desert had hardened him, and he was damned grateful for it.

"But if it was an accident…" she started.

"No. There is no excusing it." He didn't want to tell the story. Didn't want to speak of Fatin or the hold she'd had on him. About how, during a time of extreme turmoil for his country and his family, he'd only been able to think of one woman. Of how he'd wanted her.

He'd been able to spare no thought for anything else. For anyone else.

Thank God he'd cut that out of himself, that weak, sorry emotion. He'd sliced out his heart and left it to burn beneath the desert sun. Until he was impervious, until he was too hard and too weathered by the heat and wind to care about a damn thing.

Nothing but the cause. Nothing but the purpose.

And she had to realize that. She had to know. What manner of boy he'd been, what manner of man he'd become.

Why he'd had to bury that boy, deep, and destroy everything tender inside of him so that he would emerge better. So that he would never again cause such unthinking destruction.

"As with most tales, this one starts with a woman."

Ana's breath caught. She was instantly consumed with curiosity. About the woman. The one who had created emotion in Zafar. Emotion he seemed to be lacking now.

She noticed he liked to tell her things this way. As though they were nothing more than tales, and he was nothing more than the storyteller. Not a player in the piece.

"She was a servant in the palace. She had been for a long time. Beautiful, and smart. Ambitious. She didn't want to be a serving girl all of her life. She wanted more. And she was willing to do whatever needed to be done to get it. Including seducing the young prince of the royal family she served."

He looked detached, cold. Once again, this wasn't an

interaction, nor a heartfelt confession, it was a performance piece. A bit of the oral tradition the Al Sabahan people were famous for.

And yet the fact that it was personal, the fact that, though he was making the woman the star of the story, he was at the center of it, and he refused to tell it in that way, made it chilling. As cold as his eyes.

"She was his first woman. And that made him incredibly vulnerable to her. So when she asked what the new schedule was, when the sheikh and sheikha would be moved for their safety...he told her. Everything. Because in that moment, with his body sated from making love, and his heart full of hope for the future, their future, he would have given her anything she asked. And what she asked was such a small thing. Just little questions. With answers that had the power to shift the landscape of an entire country."

It was hard to latch on to the words. Hard to make sense of them. He was giving facts, honestly, but wrapped in a story, though she knew it was true. But he was holding back his emotion. Keeping it from his voice. Keeping it from her.

"Zafar...how did you...how did you survive that?"

"I wasn't the target. It was easy to get rid of me in a different way."

"I didn't mean physically."

"It was simple enough. I identified the problem, and I cut it out. Metaphorically. Were this a real tale, I would have cut my wicked heart out quite literally and left it to dry in the desert and gone on without it in my chest deceiving me. As it is, I put away feeling, emotion, and I focused on purpose. On reclaiming Al Sabah, not for me, but for my people."

"And the boy who gave it all for love?" she asked, looking at the hardened man in front of her and wondering, for just a moment, if it was even possible that the Zafar of the story and the Zafar standing in front of her had ever been one and the same.

"I left him out in the desert," Zafar said.

He'd been destroyed and remade out there. She could see that.

"Don't romanticize it," he said, his tone hard.

"What do you mean?"

"Don't lie to yourself. Don't try to make it seem like a misguided romantic gesture. It was nothing more than a sixteen-year-old boy using his balls as his brain. There is nothing romantic in that. A man in love is weak after an orgasm and she knew it. She exploited it. But there is no excusing it. She would have had no power had I been stronger. And though it's far too late to make it better, it could never happen again. Not to me. There is no allegiance I hold stronger than the allegiance I have to the people of Al Sabah. And there is nothing I would ever do to compromise it." His dark eyes glittered dangerously. "Nothing."

And she knew he meant that she would be caught up in that lack of compromise, too. That no matter what she wanted, no matter how long she was held at the palace, if it would compromise his vision for what constituted safety and success for his people, he would use her to that end.

It made her shiver inside. In that deep, endless place that Zafar's presence had created. Or perhaps, he hadn't created it; he'd just helped her discover its existence. Either way, it was disturbing, and taking up more of her than she wanted it to.

It was also far too strong for her liking.

If she wasn't careful, it might get bigger, take up more room inside. Obliterate her control. And she couldn't have that.

She had a mission. And it had nothing to do with heat and shaking and tightening stomachs.

She was going to help civilize the Sheikh of Al Sabah, and hopefully secure the future of two nations.

It really was nice to have a project. To be necessary. She knew what it was like to keep atoning.

She felt like she was still sweeping up the broken glass from something she'd destroyed years ago. And she would keep on going until she got every last shard.

CHAPTER SEVEN

Zafar had never seen so much paperwork in his life. Laws, regulations, pages of tax code, various things to look at, read, sign and start over. Every time he put a dent in a stack of papers, the pile was refreshed with more.

The air was stale. Damned stale. He wasn't used to being indoors like this. Enclosed in stone, feet thick. It was like being buried above ground. Doomed to sign his name over and over for all eternity.

In short, he was in hell.

He stood and inhaled deeply. A rush of that stale, paper-laden air hit him hard, and his stomach pitched. He wasn't used to this. He craved heat and space. He closed his eyes, but rather than the vision of the desert he expected, he saw a pale blonde with full pink lips.

He opened his eyes and scooped up his pen, and the stack of papers he was currently working on, and walked out the door of his office, storming down the corridor. Perhaps he wouldn't use an office. Perhaps he would do all of his work outside.

As if you need to make yourself appear more unconventional. Or unhinged.

He continued down the corridor and found himself heading, not toward the courtyard, or toward the front entrance, but toward Ana's room.

Flames roared through his blood, and he couldn't credit

it. He'd gone for very long stretches at a time without female companionship. In truth, his sex life had been largely dormant. He had lovers he typically managed to see once or twice a year. But there had also been times when he'd gone more than a year without making a visit.

He was past the one-year mark now since the last time he'd had sex, if he wasn't mistaken. Which could explain why that pale little temptress had burrowed her way into his mind like she had.

Just a dry spell. Dryer than the damned desert.

Emotion he'd eliminated the need for. But not sex. Still, it was rare to crave it like this.

He pushed open the doors to her chamber, like they were the flaps on a tent, without knocking. He wasn't in the habit of observing those sorts of conventions.

"Talk to me," he said, walking across the room and sitting in one of the cream upholstered chairs, setting his paperwork on his knee.

Ana was standing there, frozen, pale eyes owlish, her curves hinted at by a thin gray T-shirt and low-riding shorts that revealed the full length of her ivory legs. He wondered who had thought to provide her with such clearly Western attire. But then, there was no reason for her not to dress in the way she found most comfortable. She was in hiding from the public, after all.

"What are you doing in here?" she asked.

"I cannot abide that office. It's far too small. Talk to me while I finish this."

"What do you want to talk about?"

"I don't know. Salad forks. I don't give a damn. Let's have a conversation. I will be expected to do that in my position, I imagine?"

"Why don't we talk about why you knock on a woman's bedroom door before you enter?"

"Boring. I don't want to talk about that."

"Well, I do, I only just put my top on. I was changing."

He looked up and their gazes clashed, heat arcing between them. His blood rushed south, racing to his member, hardening him, making him ready. In case. Just in case the heat wasn't one-sided.

It didn't matter. It couldn't happen.

Somehow, it only made her seem more tempting. Only made his blood run hotter.

"But I didn't see anything I shouldn't have, so it's moot. Now talk to me."

"It's nice weather we're having. Oh, wait, except it's not, because the weather is never nice here. It's hotter than the depths of hell, and it's so dry when I went to scratch an itch on my arm I bled. *I bled*, Zafar."

"Do you require lotion? I can have some sent."

"Yes. I do require lotion," she said, sniffing. "And some nail polish. And some makeup. I received a whole new wardrobe, but not that. A flatiron wouldn't go amiss, either. My hair is rebelling against the dry."

He lifted one shoulder. "If you wish."

"I'm not usually this precious. I promise. But I'm bored. I don't want to walk around outside because it's oppressive and I don't know Arabic well enough to read the books. I suppose internet access is out of the question?"

"You suppose correctly." He looked down at the papers on his lap. "If you're so bored, use this as a chance to begin your project. Teach me civilized conversation. Tell me about yourself. I told you about me."

She sighed and shook her head, shimmering golden hair falling over her shoulders. She truly was beautiful. He could see why the Sheikh of Shakar had been so eager to acquire her, and potential oil transactions were not the only reason. Clearly.

Tariq probably thought himself to be the luckiest man

on earth. A marriage that would strengthen his country and wealth…and a wife who possessed such poise and beauty.

Truly, Al Sabah would suffer by comparison. He would never be able to find her match.

"Me? Boring. I'm from West Texas, though for most of my life I've only spent school holidays there. My father is an oil tycoon. He has a knack for finding black gold. He's mainly made his finds on private land and made both him and the landowners very wealthy—"

"I didn't ask about your father. I asked about you."

She blinked a couple of times, as though she'd been hit over the head. "Oh. I guess…people are usually very interested in what he does."

"And you spend a lot of time organizing his events and so on."

She nodded. "Yes."

"Well, let's assume for a moment that I don't give a rat's ass about oil or money. Because I don't. And let's also assume that I feel the same about power and status."

"Okay," she said, trying to suppress a smile now, the corners of her lips tugging upward slightly. She was amused and a little shocked. And he found that he liked it. Liked that he'd made her feel something almost positive.

"Now, *habibti*, tell me about you."

Because he found he wanted to know. Suddenly he was hungry for information, for every detail about her. About this woman who was so contained under pressure, who appeared soft and vulnerable, but who possessed a core that was a pillar of stone, holding her up unfailingly no matter how the sands shifted beneath her.

"Um…I went to a girl's school in Connecticut. It was very strict, but I enjoyed it. All of our focus was on education, not on boys. I came home in the summer and around holidays—"

"To help with your father's events, I would imagine."

She bristled a bit at that. "Yes."

"And where was your mother?"

She looked up, out the window. "She left. When I was thirteen."

"Where did she go?"

"I don't know. I mean…she was in Manhattan for a while. And then she was in Spain. But I don't really know where she is now. And I don't really care."

"You are angry at her."

She bit her lip, as though she was trying to hold back more words. Words she didn't think she should speak, for some reason or another. "Yeah. Of course I am. She just left."

"And without her…he had you."

"Yes. When did you get insightful?"

"I have had too much time alone with my thoughts in the past decade or so. Too much thinking isn't always good. But it does produce some insight, whether you want it or not."

"I see. And did you have any great epiphanies about yourself?" She crossed her arms beneath her breasts, and his eyes were drawn down to them. Just perfect, enough to fill his palm. He could imagine it easily, her plump, soft flesh in his hands, her nipples hard against his skin.

"Just the one," he said, his voice rough.

"And it was?"

"That I was weak." His current train of thought mocked the implication that his weakness was in the past. "And that it could not be allowed to continue."

"Is that really it?"

"That I would be better dead than as I was," he said. "Because then I could do no more damage at least. But if I lived, I could perhaps fix what I had broken. So I lived."

"I can't say I ever thought I would be better off dead, but I know what it feels like to need to fix the broken things."

"Ah, *habibti*, I know you do. But at least you weren't behind the destruction."

She blinked and shook her head. "Does it matter in the end, Zafar, who caused it? Or how big of a thing it was? Broken is broken. Someone gets the blame. Someone has to try and hold life together after."

"So, that is what you are," he said. "The glue."

"I guess so. I hope so."

"And now?"

"I'll help you hold this together, too. Whatever you need."

"Why are you so willing to help now? You sound almost happy to be a part of my civilization."

"I am. It's my…project now, and I can tell you this with total honesty—if I say I'm going to do something, I'm going to do it, and I'll do it right."

"Being right is important to you."

"The most important."

Ana was a little embarrassed by her honesty, but really, why not? He'd told her everything. Had confessed to a youthful indiscretion that had caused the deaths of his parents, for heaven's sake. Why not tell him this. She'd never told anyone, not in so many words. How she had to be good. How she had to make the right choice. How everything felt like it was resting on her all the time. How she had to make herself needed so that the last remaining people in her life didn't decide she was too much trouble.

Didn't walk away because of her mistakes.

"See, I don't think being right or good is the most important thing," he said. Zafar looked down at the paper in his lap, taking a pen in hand and holding it poised above the signature line. He signed it, then moved it to the floor, holding his pen above the bottom line of the sheet that had been below it.

"You don't?"

"No. The important thing is how it all ends. It doesn't matter how you got there."

"This from the man who rescued women from ending up in his uncle's harem?"

"This from a man who bought a kidnapped woman from a band of thieves in the middle of the desert and is holding her captive in his palace until he is certain his country is stabilized," he said, looking up at her, his dark eyes intent on hers.

Her cheeks heated. Her heart pounded hard. Anger. She was angry. That was all, because she really didn't like remembering that she was at such a big disadvantage here. She wasn't used to it. She was used to being in charge. To making things happen.

She didn't like acknowledging that Zafar held the power here. That he held the keys to her very pretty prison cell. And that he walked into it whenever he liked.

"You need to shave," she said. Because she was going to start making some rules. Because she was going to take control of her project. And if she was going to stay here, she didn't need to make it easy or fun for him.

"I need to shave?"

"Yes. You look like you just crawled out from under a sand dune, which you did." He didn't really. He looked dangerous. Wicked and sexy and a whole lot of things she didn't want to admit. "You need some polish, which is what you want me to give you, right? A polish?"

He arched one dark brow. "That is a bit more suggestive than you might have meant."

Her face warmed. She wasn't entirely sure what he was getting at. What could she possibly polish that would… Her cheeks lit on fire. "I didn't mean it that way. Stop being such a man. Must you make everything…sexual?"

"It is something men have a tendency to do."

"Yeah, well, don't."

"Why does it bother you? Because you fear I might make an advance on you?"

She shook her head. "No. I know you wouldn't." It would undermine all of his other actions. And he had a young woman right here in the palace who clearly had a crush on him. Outside of that...she imagined there were a lot of women willing to submit to the desires of the sheikh.

Oh...wow. That sentence made her feel warm all over.

"Ah," he said, his voice deep, knowing. "You fear it because you enjoy it. Either because you find it entertaining, and know you shouldn't, or because you are...fascinated by the way it makes you feel, and you really know that should not be allowed."

"Not fascinated, as you put it. Not even amused."

"I don't believe you."

"And so what if you don't? What if I was? Would it make a difference?"

She held her breath during the ensuing silence, unwilling, unable to do anything to shatter the tension that was filling the space between them.

"None at all," he said, his voice hard.

"I didn't think so. Not to me, either. We're both bound by the same thing, Zafar. The need to do right. The need to fix. Now...how about the shaving?"

He rubbed his hand over his chin, the whiskers whispering beneath his touch. "I shall order a razor."

"You're going to do it here?"

"Yes. I had thought I might seeing as you are a large part of my civilization."

"All right. Order the supplies."

Ana leaned against the sink in the bathroom as Zafar looked down at the bowl of hot lather, the brush and the straight razor that had been provided by one of his serving girls.

A tremor ran through her body when she thought of the blade touching his skin. His hands, so large and masculine, didn't look geared toward fine work like drawing a blade over his skin without causing serious damage.

"Hold this," he said, handing her the end of a leather strap. She complied and he gripped the other end, bracing the back of the blade on the surface and dragging it down the length of the belt. Then he turned it and did the same, drawing it back up. He repeated the motion, again and again, her stomach tightening with each motion.

Then he handed the razor to her. "I think it's best if you oversee the project."

"Me?"

"Yes. I am yours to civilize, and this was your idea. Complete your project."

She felt like he was challenging her. Probably because he was. And she wasn't about to back down. Not now.

"Pretty gutsy of you. Handing me a blade and asking me to put it against your skin."

"You say that as though I think you could ever take advantage of me physically."

"I have a weapon."

He wrapped his hand around her arm, pressing his thumb to the pulse in her wrist. She knew he felt it quicken, knew he could feel just how delicate her bones were beneath his hand. He was very strong, and in that moment, she was very conscious of the fact that, if he had a mind to, he could break her using only that one hand.

She might be holding a weapon, but he was one.

"Indeed you do," he said, smiling, a wicked gleam in his eye. "Frightening." It was obvious he didn't mean it.

He released her and stepped back, gripping the bottom of his shirt and tugging it over his head, pulling the breath from her lungs right along with it. He cast the linen tunic to the floor and braced himself on the sink, his hands gripping the edge tightly. She couldn't help but look at him, at the movement of his abs with each breath he took, at the dark hair that did nothing to conceal his muscles but screamed at her, aggressively, insistently, that he was a man.

Much more man than she was used to.

She swallowed hard. "Right. Great."

"I suggest you gather your courage. The last thing I need is an unsteady blade."

"I don't use a straight razor but I shave my legs every day." She crossed her arms, deciding today, in this moment, she would lay diplomacy aside and go for bold. She'd been bold once. A child who ran instead of walked. Who laughed loud and often. Who spoke her mind. Until all of that brashness, all of that activity, had driven her mother away.

Until she feared it would drive her father away, too. Or the friends she'd made in school. Or Tariq.

But none of them were here now. She and Zafar were stuck with each other. She was going for broke. "I shave my bikini line. That's delicate work. I think I can handle this."

Something dark flared in his eyes, something hot and intense that she'd never, ever seen directed at her before. Not by anyone. Not by Tariq.

And she craved it. She had craved it for a long, long time, and she hadn't known it until this moment. Until the excitement and heat of it washed over her skin, sinking down through her, into her veins, pooling in her stomach.

Her breasts felt heavy, her nipples sensitive. She was suddenly aware that she could feel her nipples. So aware of parts of herself that she'd never been aware of before. He was magic. Except that sounded too light or impossible. He was something else altogether. Something dark and rich and indulgent, creating a desire in her that she'd never felt before.

"That is all very interesting," he said finally, his tone explicit, even though his words were benign.

"Yes. Well." And after she'd just scolded him for innuendo, here she was talking about her bikini line and pondering her nipples. "Is this hot?" she asked, pointing to the small marble bowl that was full of white foam.

"It doesn't matter to me."

"It does to me," she said. "Open pores would be nice. I don't really want to scrape your skin off."

He shrugged. "You can't hurt me, *habibti.*"

"Because you're immortal?" she asked, picking up a black-handled brush with soft bristles.

"Because I have felt all the types of pain there are. There is no novelty there, nothing new. It all just slides off now."

"You're way too tall. I need you to sit."

And he did, on the tiny, feminine vanity stool that was there for her benefit. It was his own fault for insisting they use her bathroom.

It was made for a woman. This entire chamber was clearly made for a woman. Though, oddly, being in the middle of all this softness only made Zafar sexier. Yes, he was sexy, she would just admit it.

Because here he seemed rougher. Even more of a man, if that were possible.

And it appealed to her. To this new, wild piece of her that was moving into prominence.

She took a white cloth that was in a bowl of warm water and pressed it over his neck, his face, letting it sit for a moment while she took the brush and dipped it in the shaving cream, swirling in the thick foam.

"Tilt your head back." And he did. A little thrill raced through her at the sight of Zafar obeying her command.

She removed the towel, brushing it over his skin before setting it back on the edge of the sink. Then she bent in front of him, picking up the brush and applying the cream to his skin with circular motions. She could feel the roughness of the hair catching beneath the brush, could hear nothing but the sound of their breathing and the lather being worked over his face.

Her own breathing was getting heavier. Raspier. It was certainly a lot harder to accomplish the closer she got to him.

"Okay," she said. "Hold still because I don't want to be responsible for the assassination of a world leader."

He obeyed again, his dark eyes trained on her as she started to work the razor over his skin. She had a knot in her throat, in her stomach. Because it was tense work. Because she was so close to him.

She took her other hand and gripped his chin, holding him firmly and angling his head to the right so that she could get a better look at his face, so that she could skim the razor over the square line of his jaw with ease.

She dictated his movements, and he obeyed. It was an interesting thing, holding a blade against her captor's skin. And yet, that wasn't her dominant thought. It was about how near he was. How good he smelled. Like spices today. Like soap and, now, shaving cream.

"Hold really still," she said, when she got to the line between his nose and upper lip.

He put his hand on her lower back, just before the metal touched his skin. "Be careful," she said. "Don't surprise me."

"I'm bracing myself," he said, his eyes locked with hers.

She should tell him to remove his hand. But she didn't. It was warm and heavy on her body, and it reminded her of that first night in the tent. When she'd let go of all her tension and slept, rather than standing vigil. Rather than fearing for her life. When, for the first time in…maybe ever, she'd released every worry and simply drifted into deep, heavy sleep, his protective hold on her, making her feel safe.

But this wasn't a protective hold. And it didn't feel safe. Not in the least.

But she didn't stop him.

She touched the steel to his flesh and breathed out as she moved, leaving his skin smooth. Taking away years with each stroke. It was like uncovering something he left buried, pieces of him revealed before her.

She couldn't fully focus on it, or enjoy it, because his touch was sending waves of sensation through her that were impossible to ignore and that took up far more of her brain power than she cared to admit.

When she ran the blade over his neck, his Adam's apple, a shiver of that same disquiet she'd felt when he'd first pulled out the razor went through her.

"This seems very dangerous," she whispered, her face so close to him that her lips nearly brushed his neck.

"Perhaps a bit," he said, his hand sliding to her hip, his fingers digging into her, and she wondered if they were meaning the same sort of danger.

Then she had to wonder which kind of danger she'd really been referring to.

"Quite a show of trust," she said. "For a man who, I imagine, doesn't trust very many people."

She looked up at his eyes and was surprised to see confusion there. "It is true," he said.

"You trust me, don't you?"

"I have no real choice," he said. "You have the power to upend my rule. To start a war between two nations. And at the moment—" he angled his head, tilting it back so that the edge of the blade pressed harder into his skin, so very near his throat "—you have the power to end me if you choose." For a brief, heart-stopping moment she almost thought he was requesting it. As though he wanted her to do it.

Instead, she just continued her work, trying to steady the tremble in her hand, more determined than when she'd started that she wouldn't so much as graze his skin. Wouldn't spill a drop of blood.

"There," she said, her voice a whisper. She wasn't capable of more. "Finished."

She stepped back, away from him, moving away from his touch. Then she took the towel and wiped off the excess shaving cream, leaving him sitting before her, an entirely different man.

She could see him now. See that he was a man in his early thirties, handsome beyond reason. She'd known he was arresting, that he had a mouth made for sins she could scarcely imagine, but she'd had no idea he was this…beautiful.

Because this was beauty. His jaw was square, his chin strong, lips incredibly formed. The loss of dark hair on his face made his brows more prominent, made his eyes that much more magnetic.

With shorter hair, he would look even better. With nothing to distract from that perfect face.

"You are staring," he said, standing, forcing her to look back down at his bare chest. She needed to look somewhere more innocuous. Somewhere that wouldn't make her feel tense and fluttery and…sweaty.

But there was no safe place to look, except at the wall behind him. Because everywhere, absolutely everywhere, he was a woman's deepest, darkest fantasy. The kind that came out in the middle of the night when she lay in bed, restless, aching and unsatisfied. The kind that she knew she shouldn't have, shouldn't give in to.

But did. Because she didn't possess enough strength to do anything else.

"I'm just surprised at what I uncovered," she said. Best to be honest, because she didn't have the brainpower to come up with a lie.

He laughed. "Expecting hideous scars, were you? Those are just in here." He pounded on his bare chest.

"I didn't know what to expect." She swallowed. "I do think you should cut your hair, and you should definitely enlist someone other than me to do it."

"Why is that?"

"I'll answer why to both possible questions. Because you don't need to hide behind all the hair. You'll shock people more if you step out completely clean, I think. Defy expectations and exceed them—that's what you want, isn't it? And secondly, because the only way I could cut your hair is if we took the fruit bowl in my bedroom and emptied it, then turned it upside down on your head. I don't think that's the look we want."

He laughed and it made her warm up inside. "I suppose not. And I see your point about…out-polishing their expectations."

"It would be good for you," she said. "Think about it… you show up at the party in a dark suit, tailored to fit, and your hair cut short, clean shaven. You won't look like a man who's just stepped out of exile, but a man who was born to his position. Which, you are."

He shook his head slowly. "I am glad I didn't walk a straight line from the cradle to the throne. I strongly regret what happened. The loss of my parents. But without it…I would have been a weak, spoiled and selfish ruler. I fear I would have been no better than my uncle. At least out in the desert I learned self-denial. At least I learned about what mattered. It is the one good thing to result from it all. I will be better for Al Sabah because of it. Sadly, Al Sabah is starting from a place of weakness. Because of my own weakness."

"You've transcended that weakness," she said. "You've spent the past fifteen years doing it. So show them, Zafar, show them your strength. Give them a reason to stand behind you."

CHAPTER EIGHT

ZAFAR LOOKED IN the mirror, which was something he didn't particularly like to do. It was a difficult task over the past few years, as he, in many ways, hated the man he saw. Plus, it wasn't like he carried a compact in his pocket. He saw no point in owning a mirror out in the desert.

But he was looking now. He'd had a haircut, and he had shaved himself in the few days since the shave Ana had given him.

He looked very different than he'd thought he did. He'd seen himself as a boy. Since then he'd always had a beard and long hair, and he'd looked at himself infrequently.

Seeing himself without anything covering his face, his hair short, was more shocking than he'd thought it might be. He was a stranger to himself, this, admittedly, more civilized version of the man he was looking back at him from the mirror.

His appearance had never mattered to him. Every day he rode through the desert, the safety and well-being of the people there his job. His duty. If he had word his uncle's men were around then he was there with his men, preventing any injustice that might happen, by any means necessary, and then melting back into the desert as though they had never been there.

As far as Zafar knew, his uncle had never known it was him. His uncle hadn't known of his continued existence.

He was sure Farooq imagined that he'd gone back to the dust, another victim of the unforgiving desert. And that had suited him well. The Bedouins were loyal to him, above all else. And the few times he'd tangled with soldiers from the palace…

They had left no men to return with a tale.

He looked at his reflection again, caught sight of the ruthless glint in his eye. The pride. The lack of remorse. Ah, there he was. This was the man he knew.

He pushed off from the sink and turned to walk out of his chamber and into the hall. He would find Ana. He needed to see if his new appearance met with her approval.

His gut tightened at the thought of her. He'd avoided her over the past few days, and it had been easy to do so. There was a lot of work to be done, more papers to sign, people to start meeting with, scheduling to sort out. Media to speak to.

For a moment, his hand burned as he thought of how he'd touched her while she'd shaved his face. She had curves, soft and womanly. The epitome of feminine appeal. Her face had been so close to his and it had taken every bit of his self-control not to lean in and claim her mouth.

But then, he very well might have found himself with a blade pressed to his throat in earnest.

He went to her room, but she wasn't there.

For some reason, the discovery made his chest feel tight. He walked quickly through the corridor and to the double doors that led to the courtyard.

And there she was, a shimmer of gold in the sunlight, sitting on the edge of a fountain.

"Ana."

She turned and her eyes widened, her lips rounding and parting. She'd looked at him like that after he'd shaved. A look of shocked wonder. Like someone who had been knocked over the head.

It was quite endearing in its way.

For his part, were he not well-practiced in hiding his responses, he was sure he would be wearing a similar expression. Seeing her out in the sun, in a white dress that left her legs and shoulders bare, pale hair shimmering in the light, was like a punch in the gut.

Heat pooled down low, desire grabbing him by the throat and shaking him hard. In that moment, he suddenly wanted so badly to touch her skin, to see if it was as soft as he imagined, that he would have gladly sold his soul, traversed the path into hell and delivered it to the devil by hand, just for a touch. A taste.

And it would cost his damned soul, no mistaking that.

But then, as it was damned already, did it really matter?

Yes. It did. Because Al Sabah mattered. His people mattered. He was beyond the point of redemption. He wasn't seeking absolution, because there was none to be had. But he would see his people served well. That was what he intended. To lead. To lead as a servant.

Anything else was beneath him. Any chance for more gone years ago.

It didn't matter how beautiful she looked with the sun shining on her, with her hair spilling over her shoulders like a river of liquid gold. It didn't matter that her breasts were made to fit in his hands, and he was certain they were.

A man only had so much emotional currency, and his had been spent the day of his parents' deaths. He'd forfeited it. To better serve. To better make amends.

And now he simply had nothing. So he would have to look, only. Look and burn.

"You look…"

"Civilized?"

"Um…I don't know if that's the right word. You are…" She bit her lip, and he envied her that freedom. He would love to bite that lip. "Look, this whole experience is all a bit, out of time for me. I'm used to having to be appropriate and well-behaved, to…contribute and be useful. But right now I'm just going to be honest. You're a very handsome man." Her cheeks turned pink.

"I'm not sure anyone has ever said that to me," he said.

"That surprises me."

"It has been a very long time since I was in a relationship where words like that were used. It has been…it's been longer than I can remember since I told a woman she was beautiful. You are beautiful," he said.

"Me?"

"Yes, you." It was a mistake to tell her that. A mistake to speak the words, and yet, he found he couldn't hold them back.

"Now, there's something I don't hear very often."

"Now I have to question the sanity of every male you've had contact with in the past five years."

"Thank you," she said. "But I've been engaged to Tariq for four years and as a result I haven't dated. And we've mostly dated remotely so…"

"And he has not told you how beautiful you are when he's holding you in bed?" he asked, knowing he shouldn't ask, because images of her in bed, naked and rumpled, made him crave violence against the man who had just had her. And even more, it made him crave her touch.

"I…we haven't…it's been a very traditional courtship. And by traditional, I mean the tradition of a hundred years ago, not the tradition of now." Her cheeks were even darker now, embarrassment obvious.

"What a fool," he said.

"What?"

"Tariq is a fool. If you were mine I would have staked a claim on you the moment I had you within reach."

She blinked rapidly. "I…our relationship isn't like that."

"And yet he loves you?"

"He cares for me."

"And you love him?"

"Waiting doesn't mean I don't love him. Or that he doesn't love me. In fact, I think it shows a great deal of respect."

"Perhaps. But if you were mine, I would rather show you passion."

"But I'm not."

It took him a moment to realize how close they had gotten to each other, that he was now standing near enough to her that if he reached his hand out, he could cup her cheek, feel all that soft skin beneath his rough, calloused palm. A gift far too fine for his damaged skin. For his damaged heart.

"No," he said, "and you should be grateful for that fact. Your fiancé sounds as though he's a better man than I."

"I'm sure he is," she said. She raised her eyes, and they met his. "But I...I don't feel..." She raised her hand, and it was her who rested her hand on his cheek. "What is this?"

"You're touching my face," he said, trying to sound normal. Trying not to sound out of breath.

"You know what I mean, I know you do. And I know... I know you know the answer."

He did. Chemistry. Sexual attraction. Lust. Desire. There were so many names for the feeling that made his stomach tight and his body hard. But it wasn't something he wanted to expose her to. It wasn't anything he could expose her to.

She put her other hand on his face, aquamarine eyes intent on his. "I don't even like you," she said. "I think I might respect you in a vague sort of way, but I think you're hard. And scary. And I know I don't have a hope in the world of ever relating to you. So, why do I feel like there's a magnet drawing us together?"

"Is it just since I shaved? Perhaps it's that you think I am…handsome, as you said."

She shook her head. "It started before that."

"Perhaps you should discontinue your honesty," he said, his voice rough. "It will not lead us anywhere good."

"I know," she said. "I know. But…can I try this? Please? Can I just…" She closed her eyes then, blocking her emotions from view. And then she leaned in, pressing her lips to his.

It was a soft touch. But it was like touching a live, naked wire to sensitive flesh. Quick, nothing more than brief contact, but it burned everywhere. Everything.

She drew back, her breath catching, her eyes wide-open again now. And he knew she'd felt it too, just like he had. Like an electric shock.

"Does it answer your question?" he asked.

She nodded.

"And I was right. Wasn't I? It is best not to be so honest from here on out, I think."

Ana felt like she'd been singed. Her heart was pounding in her chest and she was shaking inside. Everywhere. She had no idea why she'd just done that. Why she'd touched him. Why she'd kissed him.

Only he'd walked out of the palace, looking like a fantasy she'd never known she'd had, and for a moment the entire world had shrunk down to him, her, and the way he made her feel. The things he made her want.

And she'd needed to know. Was it all adrenaline and fear? Confused by the fact that he was an appealing, powerful man? Or was it attraction. Deep, lusting attraction that wasn't like anything she'd ever felt before.

The moment their lips had touched she'd had her answer. She didn't like her answer.

She'd kissed Tariq a few times. And before that, she'd kissed three or four boys at inter-school mixers. Light kissing, with a little tongue. Some of the boys had given more tongue than she'd liked.

But this had left them all so far in the dust it almost didn't seem like it could be considered the same activity. It was so dissimilar to every other kiss she'd had, she wondered if it was something different. Something more. Or if those first kisses had been failures. But they hadn't seemed like it at the time.

She'd liked kissing Tariq. Had thought dreamy thoughts about what it would be like to kiss him more. To do more than kiss. She'd been looking forward to being his wife in every way.

And then there was Zafar. He had walked into her life and swept her up in his whirlwind, leaving so many things devastated in his wake.

"Just tell me one thing and then we'll suspend honesty on the subject," she said, fighting the urge to reach up and touch her lips. To see if they felt hot.

"I will decide if I'll tell you after you ask the question, *habibti.*"

"Okay." Normally she would be so embarrassed. Normally, she would never have kissed a man like that, and normally she would never ask the question she was about to. But normally, she lived life to keep everything around her smooth. She lived life in a calm and orderly fashion. She never ruffled feathers or made things awkward.

At least, that was what she'd trained herself to do after an act of clumsiness had resulted in her mother telling her all of her faults. All of the little ways she ruined the other woman's life. And then in her mother leaving. Because she couldn't stand to live with such a child anymore.

But in the past two weeks she'd left home to see her fiancé, the man she would marry, taking a step toward becoming sheikha of a new country, to becoming a wife. Then she'd been kidnapped. Then she'd been ransomed by Zafar and taken back to the palace and given the job of civilizing a man she was starting to think was incapable of being civilized. So she felt like she was entitled to be different.

She was starting to feel different. More in touch with the girl she'd been before pain had forced her to coat herself in a protective shell. To live her life insulated, quiet and never making waves.

Now she didn't mind if she made waves. Not here with Zafar. Here she felt bold. A little reckless. In touch with her body in a way she'd never been before.

"Is it always like that?"

"What?" he asked.

"Kissing. Does it always feel like that? And when I ask this question I'm assuming that the kiss made you feel the way it made me feel. I'm assuming it made you feel like you'd been lit on fire inside and like you wanted more. So much more it might not ever be enough. If it did…is it always like that?"

"I should not answer the question."

"Please answer."

He leaned in, resting his thumb on her bottom lip. She darted her tongue out, instinct driving her now, not thought, and tasted the salt of his skin. Heat flared in his dark eyes.

"No," he said, the word sounding like it had been pulled from him.

"No, you won't answer, or no, it's not normally like that?"

"It's never like this," he said. "I do not know how the brush of your lips against mine can make me *want* like this. Like the basest sexual act never has. But it doesn't matter."

She nodded slowly. "Yes. It matters."

"Does it change anything?"

"No."

And it didn't. But in some ways it was gratifying to know that she shared what was probably a normal level of chemistry with Tariq. That this thing with Zafar wasn't normal. That it wasn't something you were supposed to feel, that it wasn't something everyone had, that it was something she was somehow missing with the man she was going to marry.

That would have been a harder truth.

Maybe.

It wasn't actually all that comforting to know that she was experiencing some sort of intense, once-in-a-lifetime type attraction to a man she had nothing in common with. A man she could never, ever touch again.

Not if she valued her sanity. Not if she valued her engagement.

And she did. She valued both quite a bit.

"But I wanted to know because…because if it's something you feel with everyone, but I somehow don't feel it with Tariq…well, I needed to know that. But this is better."

"Is it?"

"Yes."

"I find it near the point of unendurable, and I have endured a lot. Dehydration. Starvation. All things you can forget if you go deep enough inside yourself. But this… with this, it comes from deep inside of me and I'm not certain how I'm supposed to escape it."

Ana swallowed hard, her throat suddenly dry, and she couldn't even blame the desert heat.

She looked down. "We just ignore it. There's no point to it anyway."

"None at all."

"So, in the spirit of ignoring this, you do look very civilized, but we are going to have to work on your manners."

"My manners?" he asked, his brow arched.

"Yes. What sort of dinner are you having at your big event?"

"Western-style dining."

"I thought as much, with all the ambassadors coming from Europe. How long has it been since you used a fork?"

"Certainly since I lived here at the palace. I did have some…etiquette lessons naturally, but it has been a long time since I've been expected to use any of it."

"You had to learn a whole new culture, didn't you?" she asked, realizing that royalty didn't act the same as the masses. And the Bedouin culture was different to the people in the city.

He nodded. "Yes. But I found acceptance there. And purpose. It was a place to rest and to find reprieve from the effort of existence. On your own, in the desert, survival is nothing short of a twenty-four-hour struggle. There is no end. There is no real sleep."

"I had a taste of that when I was out there. With them."

"I know you did. I wish I could have spared you that."

She shrugged. "I don't know. I wasn't hurt. Not really. Scared, but not hurt. I was lucky."

"You were unfortunate enough to get caught in the crossfire. I don't think I consider it lucky."

Except it was strange. What had happened before the kidnapping suddenly seemed the hazy and distant thing. Her whole life seemed hazy and distant. There was something so harsh and real about the light here, so revealing. It made it impossible to focus too much on the past. Or the future.

The present was far too bright.

"Well, as you said, this is pretty plush for a jail cell."

"You aren't a prisoner," he said.

"Except I can't leave."

"There is that."

Silence stretched between them.

"Dinner," she said. "Tonight."

"I shall make an effort to dress for it," he said.

"Great." She looked back at the fountain, the sunlight sparking off the water. She looked back at him and tried to breathe. It wasn't easy. "Pro-tip. The salad fork is on the left. Outside."

CHAPTER NINE

ANA FELT SELF-CONSCIOUS and a little silly. She had dressed up. Zafar had said he would dress for dinner, and because of that, she'd felt like she should, too.

So she was walking down the empty corridors of the palace in gold heels, provided by Zafar's very efficient dresser, and in a red dress that came up to her knees and draped over her shoulder like a Grecian-style gown, chiffon flowing over her curves as she walked.

She had her hair swept up into a French twist, her lips painted to match the dress. And she had to wonder why she was doing it. Why she was bothering.

Because the simple fact was, she was attracted to him. In spite of what she said about it not mattering. It was still there. And it was unnerving.

You can't do anything about it. You don't like him. And it would be wrong.

Yes. It would go against everything her father had been trying to build up. She had a flash, suddenly, of what Zafar had said when she'd told him about her father. That he wanted to know about her, not about her father.

But, her father aside, she had her commitment to Tariq. And she loved Tariq. Didn't she?

It was hard to picture him now. He was fuzzy, like there were heat waves standing in the way of her memories of him. And that was just wrong. It shouldn't be so easy to forget. Zafar's face shouldn't be so prominent in front of her mind's eye.

And she really shouldn't have put on red lipstick for the man. But since she'd complained about her lack of frills, more had been provided, and she hadn't been able to resist.

She sucked in a breath and turned the corner into the dining room. And was shocked to find it transformed. There was a formal, Western-style dining table with chairs all around it, and delicate white china place settings. It was something she would have organized for her father. Elegant and restrained, and odd in this setting because it was only for her and Zafar when it could have easily been a dinner for twenty-five.

And Zafar sat at the head of the table. He stole her breath. Her lungs contracted, the air rushing from them, and she couldn't breathe, couldn't think. She could only look.

He was sitting there in a black jacket, a black tie and a black shirt. The picture of masculine grace. The picture of civility.

Such a lie.

Because when she looked closer, at his face, the truth was plain. He was a predator, leashed and collared for the moment, by expectation, by duty. But it was only the leash keeping him from pouncing.

Were it not for the restraint of duty, he would be wholly unpredictable. Wholly frightening. A beast uncaged.

He stood, and she felt light-headed. His physique was outlined to perfection in the suit, exquisitely so. He was broad shouldered, broad chested, his waist and hips narrow. Impossibly hot.

She'd never seen such a good-looking man before. Ever. Not in the movies, not in magazines, just ever. And she knew that beneath that oh-so-sedate black jacket and shirt were muscles that would melt a lesser woman from the inside out.

Though, at the moment she herself felt a little melty, in spite of the fact that she was engaged. In spite of the fact that she knew she wanted nothing to do with him. Her fingers itched to put her hand on the knot at he base of his throat and loosen his tie.

Why would she want to ruffle him when he'd just now gotten all together? It was ridiculous.

"Good evening," he said. "I trust you found your afternoon restful?"

Restful? She'd kissed the man and spent the entire afternoon burning. "Quite," she said.

He moved away from his spot at the table and went to the chair that was positioned to the right of his own. He curled his fingers over the back of it, then pulled it out. "Have a seat."

She moved toward the chair, never taking her eyes off his face. She sat and he returned to his own seat.

"And how was your afternoon?" she asked.

"It was very good. A suit was delivered and I had it fitted to me. That was an experience I've not had for a long time."

"I imagine not."

She imagined tailored clothing was a luxury he'd been without since he'd been cast out of the palace. "Suspending with civil, bland conversation for a moment."

"You felt the need to notify me?"

"Just so you would know this isn't the kind of thing you'll talk about at your presentation."

He nodded. "All right."

"Are you ever angry?"

"Always, but about what specifically?"

"This." She indicated the suit. "This should have been yours. Always. You should have always had custom clothes and a position at the head of the table in the palace. You should have always been here, and not living out in the dirt in a tent. Doesn't it make you angry that you had it stolen from you?"

And she realized in that moment that part of the reason she was asking was because she was angry about everything she should have had.

About everything that had been taken from her because of the selfishness of others. Because of her mother. Because her mother had made her hate the girl she'd been. Had made her fold inward, smooth every rough edge. So that she would never again be in the way. Never be impulsive. Never truly be herself.

Why was she thinking about that? She'd never thought of it that way before, and now here she was having some kind of epiphany in front of an empty dinner plate with her captor to her right, looking at her like she'd lost her mind.

"I deserved to lose it," he said. "I've never been angry on my own behalf."

Neither had she. Until now.

"I'm just saying...you expect something from life. You're born into it, and it seems like you have some guarantee based on those beginning circumstances. Like... you're born into a certain family and you think...and you think you're going to have a certain future and then... you don't."

"Are we still talking about me?" he asked.

"Maybe. I don't know." She took a deep breath. "What's on the menu for the evening?" *Something bland, I hope.*

Any more excited and she was going to start saying and doing even dumber things. As if that were possible. What was it about this man? This place? It changed her. Made her say things, want things, feel things.

Maybe it was being kidnapped. She'd been freaking kidnapped, by a band of desert marauders, and she'd survived it. It made her feel stronger somehow. Made her feel like she'd found a hidden well of resilience she hadn't even known about.

But along with that, was the desire for more. Because she'd found more in herself. Because she knew there was more out there.

It was a dangerous desire. One that was coming too late. And one that really shouldn't be acted on. After all, she was under duress. And stuff.

But it was hard. So hard to ignore when everything in her felt like it was broken apart and shifted around. Like gigantic tectonic plates had shifted inside of her, creating an earthquake that wreaked havoc on her soul.

Dramatic, but there it was.

"What did you expect?" Zafar asked.

"Me? From life?"

"Yes."

"I didn't expect my mother to leave, or the way it would make me feel. Or for my father to need so much. I didn't expect for…I didn't expect for Tariq to be introduced, and for that union to be so important to…to…"

"But you love him, don't you?"

"I…yes." But for some reason the answer didn't seem as true this time. Not as true as it had seemed nearly two weeks ago when she'd been snatched out of a desert encampment and taken prisoner.

It went along with her sudden epiphany about her life growing up. With the change inside of her. What would it be like to make noise again? To stop walking so softly.

"And yet you characterize him as an unwelcome surprise?"

"Unexpected. Let's leave it at that. I just…you know, I was thirteen when my mother left. I thought I would be able to talk to her about boys. I thought that I would date. I thought I could be a kid. But…but my being a kid…that was what drove her away." She still remembered that moment, her mother, holding the broken doll and screaming at her about her clumsiness. Her childishness. "And so…I had to take care of my father and…I couldn't be another burden on his life. I had to go away to school because he didn't have a lot of time for me. I had to leave my home. And at school…they expected me to…be quiet. Be invisible. Then when I was home I had to be a hostess, as good as my mother would have been, even though I was only a child."

"Your father didn't bear his loss well."

She shook her head. "No. She was always fragile, and temperamental, but beautiful, a wonderful hostess. She liked having eyes on her, liked planning parties and organizing their social life. And she made vows to him. Of course he expected her to be there. Of course he wasn't equipped to deal with her leaving."

"And it was up to you to hold it all together?"

It was more than that. Deeper than that. But she didn't want to confess it. "Someone has to do the right thing, Zafar."

Something changed in his eyes, suddenly darker, hollower. "Yes, it's true. Someone must do the right thing even when they don't want to. Even when emotion asks you to do something differently. I never managed it. For my part, I cannot resent my lot in life because I was the cause of so much of it. Not like you. Your life has been upended through no fault of your own. And here I have only served to do more."

No fault? Maybe. Maybe not.

"Guilt, Sheikh?" she asked, her stomach tightening. Because she'd seen him look blank, she'd heard him profess guilt in a matter-of-fact manner. But she'd never heard it in his voice.

She heard it now.

"A useless emotion," he said, his voice blank now. "It fixes nothing."

"But you feel it."

"Another useless emotion to add to the day," he said, adjusting the fork on the table. "Salad fork," he said, lifting it. "Do I have that right?"

"Yes," she said, looking down at her plate. "Is dinner soon?"

As if on cue, the serving staff entered with silver trays, laying them on the table before them and uncovering them. There was rice and lamb, an Arabic feast on their Western table settings.

Like a melding of cultures. Except she felt like there was a wall between them. One that she wanted to breach now, and for the life of her she couldn't figure out why. Because she should want the wall. She should want the distance.

She was here to civilize him. Not to let him effect a change in her.

She'd spent her whole life striving to do right. To contribute rather than take. To be useful rather than a burden.

More than that, she just believed in right. In good. In doing good and being right. Because it was the best thing. It was the thing that kept the world from folding in.

It was who she had to be.

"It looks wonderful."

"Salt?" he asked.

"Oh, no, I couldn't."

"Blandness must be preserved," he said.

"At all costs. That's safe conversation."

"Ever the hostess."

"Yes indeed, but then, aren't I here to teach you?"

"You are. So I will leave it up to you to decide, then. Is it considered safe conversation to tell your hostess that she is beautiful to the point of distraction?"

"A bit too much like adding salt," she said, her cheeks heating.

"Then I shall refrain from telling you that I think your skin is like alabaster, though I think it's true. And even if there was no reason for me to abstain from complimenting you, I should never use those particular words. Because I think lines like that only seem romantic to a sixteen-year-old. Though, I think in truth I haven't made any attempts at being romantic since I was sixteen." He looked at her, his dark eyes blazing. "But perhaps it is for the best I stick to compliments of that nature. Because if I complimented you as a man…well, that would, I fear, over-salt things quite a bit."

"There's a very real possibility of that." Her pulse was pounding hard at the base of her throat, and she was sure that he could see it, almost certain that, in the silence of the room he could even hear it.

"Then I will say nothing. In the interest of safe conversation."

They'd passed safe conversation a few minutes ago. Maybe a few hours ago. And she wasn't sure what she could do to get things back on the right footing. Wasn't sure what she could do to forget the way his lips had felt beneath hers. Wasn't sure she could forget the rush of pure, unadulterated heat that had burst through her, like nothing she'd ever felt before. Like nothing she'd ever known was possible.

"I think that's for the best," she said. Then something in her rebelled, pushed her, prodded her. The deep, inner part of her, the Ana that had been repressed for so many years. "And I will say nothing about how that suit is cut so that you could almost be wearing nothing. Or maybe you'd be less indecent if you were wearing nothing. As it is, it just teases me."

"Now that, I fear, is not bland conversation in the least."

"I'm sorry. I don't know what came over me." She looked down at her plate again, then back up at him. "It won't happen again."

"I find myself disappointed by that."

"Then you'll just have to be disappointed." She sniffed and picked up her salad fork. "There is no salad."

"An oversight."

"I don't believe that," she said.

"Eat your rice with it."

She laughed. "I can't. It would be wrong."

"That will be my goal," he said, unapologetically taking a bit of rice with the aforementioned fork. "To uncivilize you a bit. A favor, as you're doing one for me."

"I'm afraid violations of table manners just can't come into it," she said, sniffing and picking up her entrée fork.

"Then perhaps we will have to think of other violations?"

She nearly choked. "Um…I think, as kind as the offer is, you have to be the focus for now."

"I don't know, in terms of needing to be uncivilized… you're about as far away from it as I am to being ready to walk into a room full of dignitaries."

"Then we'll fix that. You, I mean, not me. I don't have any wild Spring Break events coming up so it doesn't seem like I'll be needing any help with the…letting loose."

He breathed out heavily, dark eyes bleak. "And how do you propose to fix me, *habibti*?"

"You don't happen to know how to dance, do you?"

"I doubt I will be dancing at this event," he said.

"But you will eventually," she said, "and it's my job to make sure that you have adequate education in all matters of civility."

Zafar eyed the petite blonde in front of him. She was wearing casual linen pants and a loose tunic top, an adaptation of what he often wore around the palace. Though he had shown up for their dancing lesson in his suit. He felt strange about that decision now.

He had imagined she might revisit the red dress from the night before, but she had not.

"You dressed up," she said.

"It does no good for me to learn to dance if I can't manage to do it in a suit."

"I suppose that's true."

"Though I still question the necessity."

"You'll take a wife one day, won't you?"

He tried to imagine it. He had lovers, he had women that shared his bed for a couple of hours in an evening. Women he shared his body with. But that wasn't a wife. It wasn't sharing his life.

And he seriously doubted he had it in him to open himself up that much. To share all of himself. And he had to wonder what sort of life it would be for a wife. Being here in this castle, wandering around alone, going to sleep alone.

He would not share a bed with a woman, not after he slept. Because that was when the darkness crept in, unfiltered. In sleep, he had no purpose but to dream. And so he had no defense against the insidious, grasping claws of memory, guilt and unending shame.

Things he shut out in the day. Things he lived forever in the dark. His own private hell. Endless blackness. Weeping, wailing, suffering. Always.

He didn't know what he did during those dreams. If all of the screaming was in his head, or if he let it out. None of his men would have ever dared say. The desert kept secrets well.

But here? Yes, here he might truly find out the depth of the damage done. And he could very well not be able to hide it from his people.

If he let it, the enormity of everything would crash in on him. Breach the walls that he'd built up so strong, and swallow him whole.

"Yes," he said. "I will have to take a wife."

"Then you should learn how to dance. So that when you see her…across the crowded ballroom, and your eyes meet, and you make your way to her…you have something better to do than talk about the weather."

"I thought I wanted bland."

"Not with someone you're trying to know."

"Who says I need to know a wife? I simply need to marry her."

"Oh…Zafar. I only have a week left to civilize you?"

"Only a week until my unveiling. You could stay after. You might very well have to. I had thirty days, if you recall."

"I recall," she said. "Now, give me your hand."

He extended his hand to her and she wrapped her slender fingers around it, drawing him into her body. "Hand on my waist," she said, reaching down and grasping him with her other hand, putting his palm against her lower back. "And this one out."

"Music?" he asked.

"We'll count. A waltz is a three-count dance."

"A waltz? What the hell is this? A Jane Austen fantasy?"

"You know Jane Austen?"

"I have been out in the desert for fifteen years. I may have missed popular culture, but not classics."

"And you even consider her works to be classics?"

"I am a barbarian, but I'm not entirely without culture." He pulled her more tightly against him. "And anyway, one has to amuse themselves somehow." He paused, looking down at his feet. "Books were a luxury not often affordable. I came upon one, a gift from a merchant I aided. *Pride and Prejudice* in English. It is the only book I owned."

"I never…I never considered that. Not having access to books."

He shrugged. "Elizabeth Bennet is nice company. She has a sharp wit. Reminds me a bit of you."

"Oh, Zafar, you should have no trouble finding a wife."

"Although, I'm not exactly Mr. Darcy."

"Not so much."

"One, two, three," she began, her voice in staccato rhythm. "Follow my lead, one, two, three."

"I thought men were meant to lead."

"Not when they don't know how to dance. You can lead when you get this down. One, two, three."

He followed her steps, but everything in him was focused on where his hand rested, just on the rounded curve of her hip, on the brush of her breasts against his chest.

"One two three," she continued, but he could hardly hear. His eyes were focused on her lips, on the movement they made when she said the words. Numbers, an endless repetition. Something that shouldn't make a man feel anything, much less a fire in his blood that might reduce him to ash on the spot.

Blazing, hotter than the desert sun. He'd thought he'd withstood the most destructive heat in existence. In the wilderness. In his nightmares.

But this was a different kind of heat altogether. One that burned but didn't consume. Endlessly going on and on. Just when he thought the peak had been reached, it only went up higher.

Hotter.

What magic did this woman possess? Living out as he did, he could not discount the presence of the supernatural, and part of him wondered if she had some sort of power. Something to snare him.

Like a Jinn, made of smokeless, scorching fire. Whispering to his soul and telling him to commit sins he knew well he could not.

And when he looked in her eyes, he saw nothing but clear blue. It made him wonder if the desire for sin came, not from her, but from the depths of his own soul. It shouldn't be able to speak to him. It should have been choked out, dried and left to rot on the sand, along with his heart.

Both his heart and soul were so deceitfully wicked. That was why he tried to shut them down. To keep them from having a say in his actions.

When a man didn't have a trustworthy conscience he had to learn his purpose in his head and stick to it.

No matter how soft a woman felt beneath his hand. No matter how enticing the brush of her breasts, the promise of pleasure on her lips.

"Tell me something bland," he whispered, trying to ignore the burn beneath his skin. Trying to ignore the rush of blood to his groin. The ache that was building there.

"I'm counting. Isn't that bland?"

He looked at her pale pink lips. "It is not."

"I don't know how I could be more boring." She kept moving him to soundless music that must be playing in her mind, never losing the beat.

"It is your mouth," he said. "I find it distracting."

"That isn't my intent."

"Intent doesn't matter. It's the result. And the result is that I find myself unable to look away. And when I look at your lips, all I can think of is how it felt for them to touch mine."

"I'm engaged," she said, her tone firm. "Engaged and in love and…"

He pressed his lips against hers and the dancing stopped. She froze beneath his mouth, her body rigid for a second, and then it softened. Her fingers went to the lapels of his suit jacket, curling in tightly as she rose up on her tiptoes, deepening the kiss.

If there had been fire before, this was the introduction of oil. A burst of flame that threatened to destroy everything in its wake.

Her tongue slid against his, and he was pulled into the darkness. There was nothing else, nothing but the slick friction, nothing but her soft, perfect lips.

Until her, it had been a long time since he'd been kissed. Longer still since a kiss had been simply a kiss. And that simplicity gave it the power to be so much more.

He wrapped his arms more tightly around her and pulled her flush against his body, bringing those full, gorgeous breasts against his chest as he'd fantasized about doing for…had there ever been a time when he hadn't? Had there truly been a moment when he hadn't wanted her?

When he'd seen her as nothing more than a pale, fragile creature diminishing beneath the Al Sabahan sun? How had he ever seen her that way? In this woman lay the power to bring kingdoms crashing down. To bring a sheikh to his knees.

He wrenched his mouth from hers and kissed the curve of her neck, his teeth grazing the delicate skin at her throat. He pressed his thumb to the hollow there, felt her pulse pounding wildly. Felt each raw catch of breath.

He growled, his response feral, beyond thought or reason. Quite beyond civility.

She moved her hands to his shoulders, her fingers digging into his skin through the layers of his coat and dress shirt. Not enough. It would never be enough. He pulled away for a moment, shrugging his coat off and letting it fall to the floor.

Her fingers were fumbling with the knot of his tie. Of all the times, why the hell had he chosen to wear a suit now? A linen tunic was easily cast aside, robes quickly dispensed with. This Western style of dress gave no concession to lust-tinged urgency.

He struggled with the tie, and the collar of his shirt, tearing something, the tie or his collar, he wasn't sure. He didn't care. He was a sheikh. More clothes could be bought. Passion like this…it could only be taken in the moment.

"Oh…Zafar."

That, his name, seemed to suddenly knock her back to reality and she pulled away from him, struggling in his embrace. "Stop," she said, "stop."

He released his hold on her immediately, his hands at his side, his heart thundering so hard he feared it would simply stop before the next beat.

"What?" he asked, knowing he sounded angry, shocked. But he had felt, for a blissful moment in her arms, as if the blistered, hardened shell that covered him had been rolled back and he'd been exposed, new and tender, but feeling. And it had been incredible.

It had been beyond anything he'd ever before experienced, even with Fatin, who he'd believed he loved, who—damn his foolish, romantic soul—he *had* loved.

Ana's kiss made him feel like a new man.

Ana's kiss was more than he deserved.

And then the horror of it dawned on him, as the blood receded, as it went back to his brain, he realized what he had done.

Once is carelessness, twice is the measure of a man.

Or rather the foolishness of a man's measure. His body betraying him yet again. His cock controlling him.

He straightened. "Of course we have to stop."

"I'm engaged to Tariq."

An animal in him raged, wounded and seeking to lash out. "I don't give a damn about your engagement!" he roared. "The fate of a nation rests on me. Whether or not you're faithful to your fiancé is none of my concern. But war is. And I would never compromise the lives of my people, the future of my country to spread your legs. You are not so valuable as that."

His head pounding, heart threatening to burst through his chest, he turned and walked away, leaving her standing there, staring after him.

He had hurt her. He didn't care.

It was better he hurt her now. Better he hurt her this way.

Images flashed before his mind, images that were curled and burned around the edges, tinged in red. Blood soaked and inserted so deep into his mind it could never be removed.

It was this palace. These walls. That woman.

He wanted to vomit. He stopped walking and pressed his head to the wall, the cold stone cooling his blood. He stood for a moment, breathing through the nausea, through the pain that seemed to be everywhere. His mind, his treacherous member and his heart, as events from the past wove their way into the present and tangled themselves into an indecipherable mass in his mind's eye.

Violence was the only thing that stood out clearly. The reminder of why he must resist her. Of what he must spare her and all of his people from.

He pulled himself away from the wall and headed toward the gym. Simply walking away wouldn't be enough. There had to be a consequence. His body had betrayed him. And he would have to mete out punishment.

That was how she found him, two hours later. In the gym, soaked in sweat, knuckles raw, split and bleeding from punching the bag repeatedly.

"What are you doing?" she asked, standing there, feeling numb.

She was still dizzy and hot and ashamed from that kiss,

and after sulking in her room for a while she'd decided she had to go and find him and…something. Explain herself. Scream at him. Tell him he didn't know her life and he couldn't judge her.

And then she'd walked into his gym and seen him like this. Like a man possessed.

"Zafar," she said, "what are you doing?"

He looked at her this time, eyes black, soulless. He turned away, rolled his shoulders forward, sweat rolling down his back, running over sharp, defined muscles, down to the dip at his spine, just before the curve of his butt, barely covered by his descending suit pants.

He punched the bag again, a spray of pink sweat spreading through the air on contact.

"Stop!" she said, the shout torn from deep inside of her. She didn't care if she was loud. She didn't care if she was a nuisance. She didn't care if she made him angry or made herself seem less useful, or more of a burden.

She shouted it, let it fill the silence of the space.

It seemed to jolt him out of whatever world he was lost in. "What do you want?"

"Maybe you should tape your knuckles before you do that."

He looked down at his hands and lifted one shoulder. "Why?"

"So you don't turn your fists into hamburger."

"Doesn't matter."

"What do you mean it doesn't matter? What's wrong with you?"

"I deserve it," he spat.

"Why? For kissing me?"

"For endangering my entire country, yet again, because I can't seem to think with my brain." The implication was crude, and to Ana, it felt like a slap in the face.

"It only endangers things if I tell. I won't."

"It doesn't change my actions, you telling or not. It doesn't change the fact that *I* haven't."

"Were you kissing me because you love me?"

Those dark eyes swept her up and down. "No."

She nodded slowly. "I think you've changed. Granted, I didn't know the boy you used to be, but the man standing in front of me would never sacrifice anything for love. I doubt he could even feel it."

"I thank you."

"It wasn't a compliment."

"It can be nothing else to me. I have a country to defend, to take into the modern era, and I can't waste surplus energy on abstract emotions that don't matter."

"How can love not matter?"

"Why would it?"

"Because what drives you if not love? Don't you love your people?"

"I am loyal to them. I can hardly love them."

"Love is the fuel that keeps loyalty burning," she said, not sure where she'd found the strength to argue with the man standing in front of her. Because this wasn't her civilized dinner companion, or her dance partner. This was a wholly different beast. A man with scars on his skin and his soul, both cracked and bleeding. A man who radiated barely contained rage and violence.

"Is that right? Is that what keeps your engagement to your precious Tariq so strong? Loyalty fueled by love."

"No," she said, the realization creeping over her slowly. "That's not it. It's…my dad. I…I have to do this, Zafar, because *he* loves me. Because when everything in his life crumbled, when everything in my life crumbled, we were all each other had, and I feel like if I don't do this, I run the risk of losing the one person who was always there for me. The person who gave so much for my happiness."

"What did he give you, Ana? What did your precious

father ever give to you? You said yourself, you were the one who organized his life. You were the one who held it together. He sent you to school, used you as a party planner when you were home."

"He didn't leave me!" she shouted. "And you wouldn't think that would be too spectacular for a parent, but my mother *did*. So something must be difficult about me. Something must make people want to be away from me. But he stuck it out. He stayed. He gave me a home, and a place to come back to. I owe him for that."

"And you don't want to lose him."

"No. I don't. Does that make me sad and pathetic? If so then fine. But I've proven that I'm easy to walk away from, so I think I have just cause to feel paranoid."

"You are not easy to walk away from. Even a man with ice in his chest can see that."

"You walked away, too. So I think basically it's all a bunch of crap."

"I saved you. I ransomed you."

"So now you want a medal for not leaving me out in the desert with a bunch of criminals?"

"I spent the last cent I had on you. I thought it might mean something. That's all. Of course I wouldn't have left you there. I have many faults, and I am heartless, make no mistake, but I also know what is right. And *right* is not leaving an innocent out there like that."

She shook her head. "And when there's no emotion behind that kind of sentiment, it means very little. Hard to have my heart warmed when I know that moment was as fraught for you as the moment you have to choose what color underwear to put on in the morning."

He advanced on her, and she fought the urge to shrink back. She never considered herself brave. She'd never considered herself outspoken, or a fighter, but Zafar made her feel just strong enough to take on the world, somehow. Even when he was the main part of the world she was taking on.

He made her feel loud.

"Intent is irrelevant, as is emotion. Action is all that matters. Result, is all that matters. I poured my heart out to the woman I loved, because of love, and that love didn't stop her from relaying that information to the enemies of my family. It didn't stop them from brutally killing my mother and father. In front of me."

That stopped her short, cold dread making her fingers tingle. "Zafar…"

"Intentions mean nothing," he ground out. "Not when everyone is dead and you're sent out to the desert to rot. Tell me then, what did love mean? What did it fuel?"

"Zafar…"

"You can think what you want, what you *need*. But love is a trap, Ana. A lie. It is being used, in this case, to keep you in line. To manipulate you as it was used to manipulate me. That's the purpose of love."

"No. I can't believe that."

"Why? Because if you did then you would have no reason to do what you're told?"

"Because I would have nothing!" she exploded, her hands trembling, her stomach pitching. "You are the most horrible, horrible man. Stay here and pound the skin off your hands. I don't give a damn."

He advanced on her then, reaching around her waist and tugging her hard up against his body. He lowered his head, his nose nearly touching hers. "No, you couldn't. Because if you believed me…there would be nothing to hold you back, and then you might have to do something out of the box, something that takes you beyond your safe little world."

He dipped his head and took her mouth, hard and swift, his lips nearly bruising hers.

When he pulled away, she simply stared at him. She wouldn't back down. She wouldn't look away. "I have been kidnapped, then bought, dragged through this godforsaken desert back to your godforsaken castle. I have been held here against my will. I have overseen your personal hygiene and attempted to teach you to waltz. You have no right to call my world little. You have no right to imply that I am not brave. No right to imply that your words could crumble my life. I'm stronger than that. I'm better than that."

She tugged herself free from his grasp and spun on her heel, turning to walk out of the room.

"A big speech, *habibti*. And yet, you are still doing everything you're supposed to be doing. You are so well-trained."

She gritted her teeth and kept walking, trying to ignore the echo of truth in the words that settled in her bones.

CHAPTER TEN

THEY SPENT THE next several days avoiding each other. Zafar knew she was avoiding him because every so often he would be walking down a corridor and he could hear footsteps, or see a brief flash of gold as she disappeared quickly back around a corner.

It was his own fault. He had failed thoroughly in the assignment of acting civilized. Kissing her, yelling at her and then kissing her again.

But she made him feel that way. Wild, reckless and a bit unpredictable. He didn't like any of it.

But the event was tonight. His debut, for lack of a better word, and he wasn't feeling confident. Put him on the back of the horse, in the middle of the desert. Let him fight with his bare hands, to the death, any man who dared threaten his people, and he had no fear.

A ballroom and cocktail shrimp were another matter entirely.

And thanks to that article in the paper, everyone here was watching. Waiting to see if he was a madman. Or a man at all.

He supposed he had no choice but to show them.

He rolled his shoulders forward, already bound up in his tailored suit shirt and jacket. And there were ghosts here. Everywhere. He couldn't sleep at all or their icy fingers invaded his dreams.

He was starting to feel a little crazy, which was what he'd feared would become of him from spending so much time alone in the desert.

Ironic that it was more pronounced now that he was back here. Surrounded by an ever-growing staff, by civilization, by modern life, which should make things easier. Instead he saw shadows everywhere. Claws pulling him down into the abyss every time he closed his eyes. Forcing him to fight against sleep.

But he had no time to deal with it. And no interest in taking pills. They would only drag him under further. God knew if he would ever come back out of something like that.

He laughed, the sound flat and bitter in the empty corridor. He was grim today. Or perhaps he was every day.

Damn, but he was coming apart. He craved space and dry air. Not these obsidian walls that felt more like a tomb than a castle.

And then he saw her, out the window, in the courtyard, her hair like a golden flame, and he could breathe again.

He walked through the hall to the doors as quickly as possible, his heart pounding hard. He needed air. He needed to see her.

"Ana," he said, striding out into the heat. She turned, the sun catching the side of her face, illuminating clear blue eyes, and he could swear his heart started over. As though every day since he was born it had been going, steadily, enduring the beatings life had thrown his way. Now suddenly, it was back at one. New. Untarnished.

The feeling only lasted a moment. Still, the exhilaration of it lingered.

"Ana," he said again. "If you could stop being angry with me for a moment, I would appreciate it. I have a big event for myself personally and my country tonight, and I have no time for you to persist in your tantrum."

Her eyes widened. "In my tantrum? I know you didn't just say that."

"I did," he said. "And I meant it. The fate of a nation is at stake. I doubt a snit is worth the fate of a nation."

"A snit? You undermined my entire belief system and told me I was stupid and imprisoned by my notion of love."

"I didn't say you were stupid."

"Only that my worldview was."

"I didn't come here to fight."

"Oh no? Why are you here?"

"Because this damned thing starts in a little over three hours, I have additional staff infesting my castle and I have to put in an appearance that is both polished and civil and I thought you might…be available to speak to me for a moment."

"About?"

"Tell me that I can do this," he said. He hated displaying this level of weakness. This level of need. That he had to use her as an anchor for his sanity. To remind him he was a man, and that somewhere in his past he had been a man who understood these types of things. A man who could walk into a room full of people and command it, command them.

He didn't know why he thought he could get all of that from her. Except he wasn't getting it from the palace. The palace was splintering him, his mind, his thoughts. And the nights were getting so bad.

She somehow made it all seem better. She made it all seem clear. Her grace and poise made him feel like he could absorb some of it himself. Like it existed in the world and all he had to do was reach out and take it.

When he was left to himself, to his own devices, he couldn't find it.

"You need a pep talk?" she asked.

"I didn't say that."

"You sort of did."

"So, what if I do?"

"I didn't think you needed anyone. Fierce sand pirate that you are."

He frowned. "Are you joking?"

"Yes. Humor. I've even made time for it in my unexciting life. You should try it sometime."

"I've never had much time for joking. I've been too busy…"

"Surviving. Making amends. Wreaking havoc on your horrible uncle's men. I know. But now you're here. And you're going to have to play the part of suave, capable ruler. Check in your pockets for loose charisma if you need to."

He felt a laugh rise in his throat, escape his lips. "This is why I needed to see you," he said.

"Why?" she asked.

"Because you make things feel…not as heavy. You make my chest feel lighter. Breathing is a bit easier."

"You've been having trouble breathing?" she asked, the look in her eyes intensely sad.

"It's this place."

"Can you tell me? Everything?"

"I wouldn't," he said.

"Why?"

"I would hate to make your chest heavy, too."

Ana blinked, her eyes stinging. And she couldn't blame it on the sun. Something in her felt like it was being twisted, tied up in knots. Like he was holding on to vital pieces of her and manipulating them somehow.

She swallowed, then nodded. "I know. It's okay. I'm just glad I made you able to breathe. Zafar, you can do this."

"And you can't be there."

"I know."

"But I will remember this."

"Our conversation?"

"How it made me feel."

She took a deep breath. "Why are you being so nice to me? A few days ago you kissed me and then you freaked out at me and…and I don't get where we stand."

"Something about being near you…your civilization tactics have worked, clearly, and I feel more connected with that, with the more polished side of myself when I'm with you," he said, his voice rough, dark eyes compelling. "And beyond that…I want you. But there is nothing that can be done about that. I can do nothing to compromise the relations Al Sabah has with Shakar. And I can offer you nothing but an isolated life here in this glorified graveyard. I would never ask it of you. Which means the only thing that can come from my wanting you is sex. And that isn't sufficient, either."

"I know," she said. But it didn't stop her from feeling the same way. From wanting him. Even while she was still mad at him for the crap that he'd pulled the other day.

But the truth was, he was right. She'd been thinking about it, and nothing else, ever since their confrontation in the gym. And he was right.

She was afraid. Afraid of losing her father's love. His approval. And she did so much to make sure she never did. To make herself important to him so that he couldn't just leave her, too. To be quiet, to be good so that at the very least, if she wasn't important, she wasn't in the way.

And the reason things had felt so different since she'd come to Al Sabah was simple. There were no shackles here. There was no one looking at her with disapproval or expectation. She had to make her own decisions to survive, to keep sane, and there was no one to guide those decisions.

It made her see things a little bit differently. It made her see herself differently.

It made her see herself. Not as other people saw her,

but just through her own eyes. And it was different than she'd imagined. She looked at herself and saw the Stepford Daughter. Someone who was doing just as she was told so that she wouldn't make waves.

Someone who was earning favor with good deeds. And she wasn't even certain her father had ever asked for those things from her. But she'd been so afraid. After her mother left she'd wondered what she'd done to make it happen. Had been consumed with ensuring she never had to endure another abandonment like that.

And it had all made sense. Doing right kept things together, doing wrong, like her mother, made it fall apart.

She hadn't even realized how much of that reasoning was borne of fear. The fear that saying no to one of her father's requests would make him leave her. That she would be left with no one.

It made her think of Tariq. It made her question her feelings for him. Made her wonder if she was just agreeing to marry him, if she only thought she loved him, because it was the course that would make the least waves.

Because what she felt for Zafar was like nothing else ever. And no, she was sure she didn't love Tariq. Under the circumstances, that was impossible. But shouldn't a bit of the lust and need spill over to a future spouse? Shouldn't some of the heat and flame she felt for Zafar be there for the man she loved? Instead, all she felt for Tariq was a drive to cement their union. Almost like he was the finish line of her good deeds.

The thought made her feel…it made her feel frightened. And more uncertain than she'd ever felt in her life.

Like a butterfly breaking out of a cocoon. But her wings felt wrinkled and wet, and she just wanted to climb back inside and curl up. Go back to sleep. Back to feeling like security was all she needed, rather than feeling curiosity about the size of the world. About how high she could fly.

Except now it was too late to stuff herself back in the cocoon. But she wasn't ready for more yet, either.

"You'll do fine tonight, Zafar," she said. "And I really hope people realize how lucky they are to have you. I hope they feel everything you've given for them."

"What if they only remember what I took?"

And she realized she didn't have an answer for him. She was just a scared girl who had no idea what she was doing with her life, no idea what she wanted. And she was trying to tell a man who had witnessed unspeakable tragedy, who had lived his life in exile, who now had to rule a country, what to do. Trying to offer reassurance in a situation that very few people on the entire planet would ever have to face. If there was even anyone else dealing with it.

Zafar was alone. In his duty. And she couldn't walk with him. Couldn't hold his hand. Couldn't lead him in the waltz or remind him to smile.

She ached to do those things. To be there to help him. Not because it was the right thing, but because for some reason she wanted to stand beside this man while he tried to fix the broken things in his country.

"Just…" She cleared her throat. "Just make sure you use the right fork. All sins can be forgiven in light of good table manners."

"Then it is a good thing I had an excellent teacher."

If the palace empty made Zafar feel like he was enclosed in a crypt, full of people it felt like a crowded crypt, and that was even worse.

Leaders from around the world were in attendance. And some of Al Sabah's wealthiest citizens.

Tariq was not in attendance thanks to the damaged relationship between Al Sabah and Shakar. But in truth, Zafar wasn't in any way sad about it. If Ana's fiancé were present, he would feel obligated to send her back with him and damn appearances.

But he wasn't. Which meant Zafar could keep her, if only for a little while longer. Just until he had a chance to think of a solution.

Yes, because you've been working on that so diligently since you brought her here.

In truth, he knew he had not. Because he liked having her around. And if the sins of his past didn't prove what a bastard he was, then surely that did.

He affected a false smile and directed it at the very lovely ambassador from Sweden, who was currently giving him a winning smile of her own, trying to entice him to come and talk to her, he was certain.

She was lovely. Pale, with the same kind of Nordic beauty that Ana possessed. And yet, on her it was a bit too stark, unwelcoming. Looking at Ana was like stepping into winter. Crisp and clear and bright.

The ambassador started to move toward him, and he started looking for exits. Everyone wanted to talk to him. For hours now, he had been making conversation. Likely more conversation than he'd ever made in his life, and it had all occurred on one night.

He looked around the glittering ballroom, scanning the surrounding for an excuse to sidestep the woman making her way to him. He looked up, into the shadowy balconies that were set into the wall of the ballroom, and he saw a flash of red that sent his pulse into overdrive.

Ana wouldn't show up, would she? She had no reason to. She had every reason to hate him, considering the way he'd treated her a few days earlier. So then, perhaps that would be incentive for her to come, to see him make a fool of himself in front of dignitaries and kings.

He looked harder into the shadows, but didn't see any more movement. No more red.

•

He started moving toward the back door of the room, not caring how it looked. Not caring that he was surely ignoring people who wanted his attention. He was a sheikh now, after all, and it would stand to reason that he would have important business to do.

A brief flash of memory filtered through his mind.

When you see her...across the crowded ballroom...and you make your way to her...you have something better to do than talk about the weather.

It certainly wasn't the weather on his mind. He looked around him, took a sharp breath and continued on.

No one needed to know he was chasing after a woman. No one needed to know that he was following his weakness yet again.

There would be hell to pay for this, later. In nightmares. In physical pain, probably meted out in the gym. But right at the moment it seemed worth it. It seemed necessary.

He walked through the double doors and into the corridor, passing the security he hired for the event without making eye contact, as he went to the curved staircase that led up to the recessed balconies.

He put his hand on the railing, his fingers sliding over smooth, white stone as he made his way upstairs. He listened as intently as he could, keeping his footsteps silent. Wondering if he might hear the whisper of her gown's fabric. Hear her breathe.

He heard footsteps, and then, a soft, warm body collided with his with a muffled "Mmph."

He reflexively grabbed the person by the arms and held them out, steady, so he could get a look. "Ana," he said.

"Guilty."

"You aren't supposed to be here," he said.

"I know, but I had to make sure you were doing okay."

"And what did you observe?"

She lifted her chin. "You're the best looking man in the room."

"That, my dear, could be construed as non-bland conversation."

"I know. I don't…I don't think I care."

"Ana, you don't know what you're inviting."

"I probably do. I think…Zafar…I've been thinking. But I don't want to talk just now." And then she was leaning into him, soft lips pressing against his. His body was on fire in an instant, all caution, all common sense gone as her tongue traced the seam of his mouth gently.

He opened to her, and let her explore, let her take.

Because he was powerless to do anything else.

"Do you have any idea what you're doing?" he whispered.

"No," she said.

Ana had to admit it, because it was the truth. She didn't know what she was doing. She'd never kissed a man quite so passionately. She'd never wanted a man with quite so much ferocity.

She'd known she couldn't show her face at the party. She wasn't supposed to be here. No one could ever know she was here.

But she hadn't been able to resist. She'd put on the red dress she'd worn to dinner. And eventually she'd gotten up the courage to slip up to the balcony to catch a glimpse of him.

No one would recognize her, even if they saw her. Not from that distance. At least, that had been her reasoning.

Now there was no reasoning at all. She hadn't planned this. She hadn't expected it. She had no idea what it would mean for her future, or why she was taking such a chance. She only knew that she couldn't seem to stop herself.

That she didn't want to stop.

That for the first time in longer than she could remember she wasn't getting tripped up pondering the whys and why nots of every action she performed. That she wasn't worrying about what other people would think. Or what they might wish she would do differently.

How could she worry about it when nothing had ever felt so right? When the press of his mouth against hers seemed essential?

And then she found herself backed against the hard stone wall, the cool rock at her back, the heat and hardness of Zafar in front of her. She wrapped her arms around his neck, clung to him, poured everything she had into the kiss.

Desperation. Passion. Confusion. Anger.

She felt all of it, swirling inside of her, creating a perfect storm of emotion that seemed to push her harder, faster.

She was so consumed with it, with him, that she hardly realized her fingers had gone to the knot of his tie. That she was loosening it, tugging it from around his neck. That she was working the buttons on his shirt as quickly as possible.

She didn't realize it until her hand came up against hot, bare skin, rough chest hair that tickled her fingertips as she swept them beneath his collar so that she could get closer to him.

He kissed her hard, pressing his body to hers. And she could feel the hard ridge of his arousal against her thigh, evidence of how much he wanted her. That she wasn't feeling this alone.

And she wanted to weep with the triumph.

Because someone felt passion for her. Because even if Zafar only wanted sex, and her body, she was certain it was more need than anyone else had truly felt for her in years, if ever.

Her father wanted her to help him maintain the status quo. To help him shore up his profits. Tariq wanted her for a revenue increase to his country.

No one wanted *her*. And no one was honest about it.

Except that wasn't true now. Zafar wanted her. And if there was one thing she knew, even with her near nonexistent experience with men, it was that erections didn't lie. It was blunt, brutal honesty at its most basic and she reveled in it.

She arched against him, pressing her aching breasts to his chest, her heart thundering so loud and hard she was certain he could hear it, certain he could feel it.

He abandoned her mouth and kissed the side of her neck, her collarbone. The curve of her breast revealed by her dress.

"This is a beautiful dress," he said. "But it doesn't give me enough of you."

He reached behind her and tugged at the zipper tab, pulling it down and loosening the dress so that it hung off her curves. Then he pushed against the single strap that held it up and it fell to the floor, leaving her standing there in a darkened stairwell in nothing but a black strapless bra and matching panties.

If she'd been thinking clearly, she probably would have protested, or expressed some form of outrage. But she wasn't. So she didn't.

He put his hands on her waist, ran his fingertips over the line of her spine. The action, so simple, so seemingly sedate, sent a riot of need through her that made her breasts ache, made her slick between her thighs.

She'd never known what it was to want a man. Not like this.

He pressed a kiss to the valley between her breasts, then traced a line there with the tip of his tongue. And she shivered.

She laced her fingers in his hair, wanting to hold him there forever, wanting to tighten her hold and tug him back up to her lips so she could kiss him again.

She just wanted. With everything in her, with her entire being. And damn anyone else's opinion. Damn the consequences. Damn quietness.

He raised his head and kissed her again, and she made quick work of the rest of the buttons on his shirt. She pressed her palms flat against his hard, muscular chest, sliding her hands downward, to his stomach.

She'd never seen a man who looked like him. He'd completely shocked her the first time she'd seen him without a shirt. Bronzed and chiseled and so sexy it nearly hurt.

She'd never noticed how sexy men were because she'd never let herself see. Because she'd been so committed to an ideal she'd shut that part of herself off and channeled controlled bits of it to the "appropriate" place.

This was like a dam burst, and there was nothing appropriate about where her desire was being channeled. And she didn't care. Not in the least.

All that mattered was how amazing he felt. How right it felt to have his lips against hers. How she felt like she would die if she didn't have more of him.

All of him.

"I want you," she said, the words torn from deep inside of her, from a place she hadn't known existed. One filled with passion, with desire that stood apart from expectation and judgment. A place that was all hers.

And, in this moment, Zafar's.

He put his hands on her lower back, pushed his finger down beneath the waistband of her sheer black panties, the reached in farther, cupping her.

The intimate contact shocked her a little bit, but not enough to make her stop. And then he dipped between her thighs, his fingers skimming her slick folds and she jumped, arching into him.

"Shh," he said, kissing her, cutting off the strangled cry she hadn't realized had been on her lips. "It's okay. Do you like it?" He stroked her slowly and her whole body shook, internal muscles she'd been unaware of until that moment contracting tight.

"Yes," she whispered, letting her head fall back. He kissed her jaw, her neck, and pushed a finger into her, slowly. Her breath caught and she held on to his shoulders.

"Still good?" he asked, pressing deeper, moving one finger farther forward to her clitoris as he stroked in and out of her gently with another.

"Yes." She closed her eyes and leaned into him, widening her stance so he had easier access to her body.

She shuddered as he continued to subject her to sensual torture with his hands, his lips hot on her neck, his tongue sliding over her tender skin.

Everything in her went tight, so tight she could scarcely breathe. She thought she would break. And just when she thought she couldn't endure anymore, his final stroke over the sensitized bundle of nerves made everything in her release.

It was like chains that had been holding her, for months, years, all of her life, had suddenly let go. And she was falling, weightless, pleasure coursing through her body. And there was nothing, no thought, no worry, no fear of judgment, or anything else.

Nothing but the white-hot pleasure that burned on and on, leaving her scorched, but unharmed. Leaving her new.

Like a phoenix from the ashes.

And for one whole minute, as she rested against his chest, her breathing returning to normal, she felt stronger, more sure, than she ever had before.

But the minute passed too soon.

And then she realized she was in a stairwell in nothing but her underwear, and she'd just let the man who was holding her captive, the man who was not her fiancé, bring her to orgasm with his hands.

There weren't enough swearwords. There really weren't. So she went through them all in her head. Twice.

And then she said one of them, the worst one she could think of, out loud because why not? Only Zafar was here. And he had just seen the most shameful, embarrassing moment of her life. She didn't have to worry too much about manners in this case. Especially not when he was holding her half-naked body against his.

But he was the one who drew away suddenly, his dark eyes haunted, his hands shaking as he pushed them through his hair. He was pale, a sheen of sweat on his gray-tinged forehead.

"I…I am sorry. Forgive me." And she was pretty sure he wasn't talking to her. "Forgive me," he said again, buttoning up his shirt as he walked down the stairs, away from her, leaving her standing there staring after him, her body buzzing, her head pounding. Her heart aching.

What had she done?

She dropped down to her knees, her legs too weak to hold her up.

"What did you do?" she said out loud.

She shifted so that she was sitting, her back to the wall, and she picked up her dress from the ground, sliding it onto her lap, holding it up over her breasts. A tear slid down her cheek. She hadn't even felt tears building, but they were here, and they were falling, faster than she could wipe them away.

If her father knew, if Tariq knew, they would hate her.

And everything would be for nothing. Her whole life, all that quiet, would be for nothing.

She scrunched her face up, lights filtering in from the ballroom below splintering and turning into glittering stars, fractured by her tears.

What had just happened with Zafar had been the single most beautiful moment in her life. In his arms she'd felt alive. She'd felt more like Ana. The Ana who was waking up from hibernation. The Ana she might have been if life really did come with a guarantee.

If she'd been free to grow up without all the baggage. Without all the fear and anxiety that one wrong move would see her abandoned by both parents.

But the beauty of the moment withered and died quickly. And it left behind the reality. She had betrayed the man she'd promised to marry. She'd done what she wanted to do, instead of doing what was right.

And she feared that, just like her mother's priceless porcelain doll, everything was too broken to be put back together.

That she had, once again, cut the tether that held the people she loved in her life.

It couldn't happen again. She could never speak of it. She couldn't even remember it. She would weather the rest of her captivity, and then she would go back to Shakar. Back to Tariq and her father.

They would never see how badly broken she was inside. And everything could go on as it was supposed to.

There was no other option.

CHAPTER ELEVEN

"WE HAVE TO LEAVE."

Zafar's voice pierced her sleep-fogged brain. She looked out the window and saw that it was still gray out. Ana rolled over in bed, put her hands over her face. "Right now?"

"Yes," he bit out. "Now."

"What about liaising and being diplomatic?" Cold dread washed over her and she sat upright. "Unless you talked to Tariq."

"No," he bit out, "I didn't. But I have been awake all night and I have decided that you failed in your task."

"I...failed." The words sent a cold stone of dread sinking down into the bottom of her stomach. So strange, because it shouldn't matter if Zafar thought she'd failed at something. But failing, being wrong, being worthless, was such an ingrained fear that no matter who spoke, the words had the power to wound her. "Why? What did they say about you? What did they say about the ball?"

"Oh," he bit out, "they loved me. They've called Rycroft a flaming idiot and said that he was slandering me in his article. Suave, they said, and handsome. But, Ana, I am not civilized, no matter what they say. And that was your job. To civilize me. And you did not. Why else would I be keeping a woman locked in my palace, keeping her from her father, her fiancé, giving no notice that she wasn't dead, rather than sending her straight back to her home, regardless of the fallout? There is no honor in that. No civility."

"Zafar…you did what you had to do."

"Stop it," he growled. "Stop trying to placate me. Stop trying to smooth things over. Some things cannot be fixed. Some things are not in your power to repair." He paced at the foot of her bed, frightening and mystifying in his anger. "Do not absolve me. It is a heresy. You don't know the sins you're trying to forgive."

"Fine. Stay in your self-imposed hell then, Zafar Nejem. I don't care. But make good on your word and take me back home. You can castigate yourself for all your wrongdoing on the way."

She flung off the covers and got out of bed, realizing she had nothing to pack. That nothing here was hers. That she would leave everything, including Zafar, behind and there would be no evidence that she was ever here. No evidence he had ever been part of her life.

That he'd been the first man to kiss her passionately. The first man to touch her intimately. The first man to give her an orgasm.

The first man to make her wonder if there was more to life than she was allowing herself to live. The first man to make her want to stand out in the open and scream at the sky so people would know she was there. So she would stop just blending in.

And she would just leave it. Leave him. It would be nothing more than a blip on the radar of her life. A couple weeks out of time, with nothing more than the life she'd led at home with her father coming before, and nothing but her marriage to Tariq after.

All the anger drained out of her, leaving her lips feeling cold. Leaving her feeling dizzy.

"That is the question. Commercial flights to Shakar

were barred during my uncle's rule. If I fly you there, we may create more of a spectacle than we would like."

"Take me back the way we came in," she said. She pictured it then, the journey to the palace on the back of his horse, the wind, harsh and arid and clean in her face.

"On a horse?"

She nodded. "Yes. No one will have to know. Leave me where I was taken. I'll lie about what happened."

"It's not so simple, and you know that. Were it that simple we could have done that from the beginning."

"I know. But...I'll lie to buy you time. Or I'll tell Tariq how you saved my life, but I'll make sure that I express nothing but deep gratitude to you and to the people of Al Sabah. I won't let there be a war."

She didn't know where the strength was coming from. She'd always liked to fix things. Had always tried to take a chance at reclaiming her life. At fixing what she'd broken.

So odd how, in all ways, she saw Zafar in herself. Guilt, blame and shame, a constant companion, and the need to try and remake everything, make it new again, fix the damage caused by their actions, an ever-present drive and burden.

But this was different. This was true conviction. A vow she was making to him that she would keep no matter what.

"Trust me," she said. "I'll fix it."

"Why do you want to do it this way?"

"Because...because I need to finish my adventure before I stop having them. Especially sad since this was my first one."

"Is that what this has been for you, *habibti*?" he asked. "An adventure?"

She shook her head, her throat tightening. "No. It's been more than that, but I'm not sure what to say. I don't even know what I feel."

He let out a heavy breath, then straightened, every inch the commanding king. "Dress yourself. Pack adequate clothing for three to five days of travel. The desert is unpredictable and often there are obstacles that prevent things from going as quickly as we might like."

"Sandstorms."

"Yes. But you will be with me. I will not let any harm come to you." She felt like he was talking about more than just the desert. Like more than just physical harm. "I promise you that."

"I believe you."

"I will gather tents and food. It will not be as rough of a journey as it was coming here."

"And will you bring servants?"

Their eyes locked, tension crackling between them, and the despair she'd felt last night in the stairwell was burned away by the heat that ignited in her veins. "No," he said. "It is best not to involve any more people than necessary."

She nodded, feeling like a hand was tightening around her throat. "No, that wouldn't do."

"Not at all."

"I'll get ready, then."

"I will wait out in the courtyard. No one can see us leave. There is still extra staff here. People who are not mine."

"I understand."

He nodded once and turned and walked out of the room, leaving her standing there, feeling like, yet again, her life had been turned completely upside down.

Strange how she was coming to expect it. How it seemed to jar something loose in her. How she sort of enjoyed it.

Well, it was coming to an end now. Because she was going back to Shakar. Back to Tariq.

She sucked in a shaking breath and started looking for a bag to pack her clothes in.

* * *

"Ready?" Zafar looked down from his position on his horse, his face mostly covered by his headdress.

She nodded her pale head. She looked…different. There was a quiet strength to her posture, her hair drawn back into a tight bun. He had always seen her as extremely self-possessed, the exception being the brief emotional meltdown she'd had when he'd first rescued her from her kidnappers.

But now she was somewhere beyond self-possessed. She had a core of steel, and he could see it. Could see that she wouldn't be bending. But he didn't know what she'd set her will to. And that was the part that concerned him most.

Aside from what being alone with her might do. Aside from what his own intentions might actually be. God have mercy on his tattered soul.

Last night he had been inexcusable with her. And no mater the outcome, he had to return her to her fiancé. To her father.

He had been wrong to keep her.

And he had been more than wrong to touch her. In that moment, when he'd pressed her against the wall and kissed her, when he'd put his hand between her thighs and felt all of her heat about his fingertips…he'd been conscious of the gates of hell opening up behind him, the flames licking his back, demons threatening to pull him in.

But not before they'd spurred him to commit the deadliest sin possible. A fitting end to his life. Except it wouldn't really be the end. He couldn't even count on being dragged into the comparable bliss of hell.

He would have to stay in this life and deal with consequences. Yet again.

Consequences he'd earned with his libido, with his disgusting lack of control. Control he'd thought he'd found out in the desert, deprived of every good thing. But back here, back where he'd started, he seemed to lose all the strength the desert had infused in him.

This, then, would be the test.

He reached down. "Need help?"

She shook her head and approached the horse, putting her small bag of clothes into the saddlebag with his other supplies before pulling herself up behind him onto the horse, wrapping one arm around his waist, her thighs bracketing his, her tempting heat against his back.

Soon the desert sun would block that. Would make it impossible to distinguish her body from the arid air.

He took the head scarf from his lap and handed it back to her. "Take this, *habibti*. You need protection from the sun."

She said nothing, but she took it from him, and the movements behind him seemed to indicate that she was following orders.

She wrapped her arm back around his waist, leaning forward, her chin digging into his back. The contact, and the pain, soothed him.

"Let's go," she said.

His agreement came in the form of spurring his horse on and heading toward the back gate of the palace. Out into the desert.

Here, he would find his salvation or his damnation.

And he wasn't entirely sure which one he was hoping for.

He didn't push his horse the way he had that first day they'd met. Instead, they rode at a more decent pace, and they arrived at the oasis just as the sun was becoming too punishing for her to endure.

"We'll stop here," he said, indicating the outcrop of rocks. "There is water just behind the rocks. I'll set up the tent there. Under the trees."

He got off the horse, and she dismounted too, pausing to stroke the beast's nose. "He needs a name, Zafar."

Zafar turned and looked at her, brow raised. "Why?"

"Calling him *horse* is stupid. I don't call you Grumpy Man, do I?" Approaching the subject of the horse's name was easier than confronting what had passed between them last night.

Thinking about the horse's name was easier, too. Which was why she'd spent the silent ride to the oasis pondering that instead of how being in his arms had felt. Of how hard and muscular he was, and about just how much she'd enjoyed contact with that hard muscular body last night.

Yes, thinking of a name for the Horse was much safer.

"I was thinking Apollo," she said, following Zafar to the oasis, where he was headed, bundled-up tent in hand.

"Why?"

"It's transcendent. Godlike."

"He is neither."

"Excuse me. Are you maligning the noble steed carrying us through the desert on its back?"

"I'm hardly maligning him. I just don't think it's a good name for him."

"You've had him for how long?"

He tossed her a quick glance before setting the tent down by the water and continuing on in his labor. "Nine years."

She shook her head. "And you haven't named him. Any name is better than Horse."

"Not Apollo."

"Achilles. Archimedes. Aristotle?"

"Why Greek and why all with *A?*"

"He seems Greek. And also I'm moving alphabetically."

"He is an Arabian horse. He should have an Arabic name."

"All right, name away."

"Sawdaa. Means black."

She crossed her arms beneath her breasts and didn't bother to keep herself from looking at his backside while he worked on the tent. "Original."

"Better then *Horse,* yes?" he asked, finishing with the tent's frame.

"Barely."

"All right then, what would you call him? Not the name of a Greek god, demigod or philosopher, please."

"Since you said *please.* How about Sadiqi. Friend."

"I know what it means."

"Well, he's your friend."

"He's my horse."

"You love nothing, Zafar? Nothing at all? Are you so determined to keep it that way that you can't even name your horse?"

He straightened and shot her a dark glare. "You know nothing about what I've been through. Telling you…it doesn't make it real for you. You don't know what I had to do to survive. To move forward. To make myself a valuable person."

"I admit," she said, walking down to where he stood and taking a position beneath the shade of a palm, "my life story has less blood spilled than yours. But I know what it's like to try to change yourself so you can have some value. I know what it is to break everything."

She closed her eyes and leaned her head back against the tree as she let her least favorite memory wash over her. "I ran through my mother's sitting room. She had her own sitting room, a parlor for entertaining her friends. And she kept her collection of antique dolls in there. She loved them." She swallowed. "I was always loud. Brash. And I moved too quickly. So one day I ran through her sitting room and I knocked against the doll cabinet."

She could still remember the little sandy-haired doll

tipping off the shelf, landing wedged between the locked cabinet door and the shelf. And she'd prayed so hard that it wasn't broken.

Her mother had come running in and opened the cabinet, and pulled out the now-hollow-faced doll, the porcelain reduced to dust on the bottom on the ground.

"I broke it," she said, trying so hard not to picture the look on her mother's face. Trying and failing. "My mother said...she said I was making her crazy. That I was always ruining things. That I'd ruined everything. Ruined things she'd loved." She swallowed the lump that was building in her throat. "I don't think I was one of the things she loved anymore."

Ana breathed in deep. "She left the next day. I'm twenty-two years old, and I know my mother didn't leave me because of a broken doll. I know there were other things. I know she probably had some problems. But then...then all I could think was...if I were more careful. If I had taken more care to listen to her, to move slower. Maybe be quieter and more poised. More helpful....if I had been those things she wouldn't have left. And if I wasn't careful...maybe my father would leave, too. After all, I ruin everything."

Her voice choked off. She hated this. Hated that she was doing this now, with him. But this was the truth of it. The truth of her life, that she hid behind fake smiles and feeling polished and pulled together.

She'd pulled her hair into a bun and learned how to say yes to everything, to be efficient, to do what was expected of her.

"You do not ruin everything," he said, his voice rough. Then he swore, vilely, harshly. On her behalf. It made her stomach tighten.

"Zafar..."

He crossed to where she was standing, every inch the desert marauder he'd been when she'd first met him, only a small wedge of his face visible, the rest concealed by his headdress.

He tugged the bottom of it down. And she saw the difference from the first day she'd met him. His clean-shaven jaw. She'd done that. She'd changed him, at least on the outside.

It made her feel strange. Powerful.

"You did not make her leave," he said. "My mother was taken from me by death. No force in heaven or hell could have removed her from me, no matter my behavior, had she been given a choice. And it is not because I was a better son than you were daughter. I was dissolute. Lazy. Obsessed with women, sex. And yet she loved me, because of *her* heart, not because of mine. Your mother's rejection… it was not because of you. It was her heart, *habibti*. It was her heart that was damaged, not yours."

"You say that but…you claim you don't even have a heart. How do you know all this?"

"Because," he said, his voice hoarse, "these past years my emotions have been dried out, unused. Dead. If anything on earth would make me wish to have them back… Ana, it's you."

A tear rolled down her cheek and she didn't bother to wipe it away. She had always tried to be who she thought she had to be. Had always tried so hard to be perfect.

But with Zafar, something in her was unleashed. The wild child she'd been born as, maybe. The girl who'd run through the halls of her family home, who'd liked to laugh and be silly. Who hadn't trembled at the thought of having a grade point average that dipped below perfect. Who hadn't been consumed with making sure she improved every situation, rather than being a bother.

She'd constructed a shield for herself. So perfect and shiny. And she wanted it gone now. She didn't want to be the person she'd built herself to be. She wanted to be the person she was born to be.

She remembered her despair last night after their near-lovemaking session in the stairwell. It hadn't been because she was sorry. It had been because she was afraid. Afraid of wanting something for her, something that her father wouldn't want for her.

And Tariq…clearly she had to examine her options there. She did not love him. She'd never been more certain of that. She'd wanted to marry him just to please her father; she'd just been too stubborn to acknowledge it.

Right now, she knew what she wanted.

"Zafar," she said, her voice a near whisper. She cleared her throat. She wasn't going to ask for this with any shame, any embarrassment. "I want you to unmake me. Out here. Just like it happened for you. I don't want to be who I was. I don't want to be weak. I don't want to be quiet. I don't want to live for anyone else. I just want…Zafar, I want. For me. Please…"

"You want to be…unmade?" he asked, his voice rough.

"That's what you told me the desert did for you. That it took the boy you were and made you the man you were. That you had to unmake yourself so you could reemerge the man you needed to be. I need that."

She pushed away from the tree and closed the distance between them. "I have spent so much of my life walking on tiptoes. Trying to be the person I thought I needed to be in order to be bearable. But it's not bearable to me anymore. I don't like me. I am trained to do as I'm told, and that day in the gym…you were right about me, Zafar—I dare not step out of line because I'm afraid if I do my father, or my friends, or the teachers I had who were more like mentors, that they would decide I wasn't worth the trouble. So I made myself indispensable to them. Want to plan a party? I'll help. Need me to marry a sheikh so you can secure easy access to oil? I can do that, too. I'll even do my best to love him. So…no one could get rid of me because I made everything easy for them."

"Except me," he said. "You don't make my life easier. You make it a damn sight harder."

"I'm glad," she said. "I'm…I'm so glad. And I know you want to get rid of me, but honestly, I can't blame you."

"Circumstances being what they are," he said, his voice rough.

"Yes. Naturally."

"How would I go about unmaking you, *habibti*?" he asked, his tone lowering, dark eyes intense on hers. She looked away, her breath coming in short, uneven bursts. "Ana," he said, his voice surprisingly soft. She looked back at him.

Then she turned away, running to the edge of the water. And tilted her head back, the sun scorching her face. She opened her mouth and took a breath, air burning all the way down.

And then she screamed. Her voice echoing all around them. Her. Ana. She was here. She wanted to be heard. She wanted to make a sound. Make an impact that was bigger than the dreams of other people. Have a life that meant more than serving the desires of other people.

Then she turned, shaking, her throat raw, and walked back toward Zafar, his expression looking as though it was carved out of stone.

"I don't want to be quiet," she said.

"And so you are not."

She shook her head. "No. I'm not. And I want…I want more than that even." She met his eyes, dark and intense. "Make love with me."

"Ana…I can offer you nothing. Nothing beyond a physical encounter. Is that really what you want?"

"Yes."

She debated whether or not to tell him she was a virgin. And decided against it. Because, given her very obviously inexperienced kissing technique, he'd probably guessed. And she didn't want to bring it up and make things any more awkward than they were.

"Why would you want me?" he asked. "I am a great sinner. Responsible for the near fall of a nation. Plus, I have not treated you admirably."

On that, she would give him total honesty. He was giving her honesty, the look in his dark eyes haunted. He needed to know why she would choose him, and she had so many reasons.

"Because, before you…I can't remember the last time I felt this way. Not just the desire, the sense of wildness. That's what it is, Zafar. I've felt from the moment I first met you that you'd opened up this part of me I'd tried to choke out. A part I'd thought just didn't exist anymore. But I was wrong. It's the part of myself I closed off. Because I was afraid of being rejected. But I wasn't afraid with you. Mainly because I wanted you to let me go." She laughed. "I didn't have to please you and I just pleased myself and I found this part of me I'd buried. A part of myself I'm so glad to have back."

She put her hand on his cheek. "And as for the desire… I've never known anything like this. I don't want to go my whole life without exploring it."

"Attraction is easy enough to come by. You will find it, maybe with Tariq."

"Not like this," she said. "Tell me honestly, and then I'll leave it alone. Has another woman made you feel the way that I do? You told me this wasn't normal. That this was stronger than most lust. It must be, because I spent most of high school being a paragon, focusing on school and things that made me…useful. And then even more in college because of Tariq, because of that alliance. Even my

major, International Studies…it was all for the future with
him. To be useful in that future and that meant forsaking
anything else. But I can't ignore this, and that right there,
that says something. But if it's not the same for you, then
tell me. And maybe I can let it go."

He looked away. "I have never felt this before."

"Then take me," she said. "Have me. Give us both this
gift."

"I cannot," he said, the denial dragged from him.
"Whether you like the idea of it or not, according to custom, you belong to the Sheikh of Shakar, and my taking you is grounds for war. I have caused a war because
I couldn't resist a woman. I caused death and destruction
because of my lust."

"But I don't want to manipulate you. I just want you,"
she said. "I have belonged to other people for a long time.
Tonight…I don't want to be Tariq's property. And I don't
want to be yours. I want to be mine. And I know what I
want."

He growled and dipped his head, kissing her hard and
deep, swiftly, pulling away from her abruptly. "Be sure," he
said. "Be very sure, because I can't stop myself. I am shaking, down to my bones, Ana. For you. Because of you."

Her heart tightened, ached. "I'm sure," she whispered,
kissing him. "I'm sure."

"I am so glad I don't have to make conversation about
salad forks now. Because all of those times, what I wanted
to say was that you were beautiful. That I wanted you to
the point of distraction. That your body is enough to make
grown men drop to their knees and give thanks to God
that they were born men. I wanted to tell you that your red
dress should be illegal. That taking it off you was one of
the single greatest privileges I'd ever been given. But of
course I could not, because I was relegated to the bland.
But not now."

"No. Not now. Now I just want you. All of you."

"You don't know what you're asking for," he said, tracing a line over her cheekbone with his fingertip, down to her lips.

"Then show me."

"Ana…"

"Zafar, what do you see when you look at me?"

"Beauty," he said, without hesitating.

"Anything more?"

She looked in his eyes, and she realized she didn't need more. He was here, putting everything on the line for her, betraying himself for the passion that had ignited between them.

There was heat and sand and Zafar.

Everything else burned away.

"There is so much more," he said, his lips on her neck, her collarbone, his hands tugging at the hem of her shirt, drawing it up over her head. "So much," he said, pressing a kiss to the curve of her beast, just above the line of her bra.

"Show me," she said, lacing her fingers in his hair, fighting the release of the sob that was building in her chest, pressure so intense she was afraid she might burst.

He stepped away from her and turned, his back to her, his eyes on the water in front of them. And then he reached in front of his body and started working the tie on his robes, divesting himself of the layers, placing them on the sandy ground, until he was completely naked.

Her breath caught, choked her. She'd never seen a more beautiful sight than the view of him, lit by the sun, his shoulders broad and powerful, the muscles in his back sharply defined, his waist trim, dimples just above his truly glorious butt, round and muscular and just everything she thought a man's backside should be.

And when he turned, she was certain her heart stopped. He was really, well and truly beyond her experience. She'd never seen a naked man in person. She'd seen limited pictures of the male member. But hadn't seen much in the way of erect men. Unwanted spam emails, the contents of which she always closed her eyes against and deleted as quickly as possible, hardly counted.

A textbook drawing outlining the different parts of male anatomy also didn't count.

He was much larger than she'd imagined he might be, but she wasn't worried. She knew that generous size was supposed to be a good thing. So she was fairly certain that, first time, mandatory pain notwithstanding, his proportions were an asset to her.

He made his way back to her and took her hand, leading her to where he'd left his robes laid out on the sand.

He pulled her down to the soft ground with him and pulled her into his strong arms, stroking her hair as he kissed her, as he held her up against the hard, bare length of his body.

She wrapped her arms around his neck, tangled her legs, still clad in jeans, with his. He put his hand on her back, spread his fingers wide over her skin before grasping the clasp of her bra and releasing it, pulling the undergarment off and tossing it aside.

He continued to kiss her, not giving her a moment to be concerned about her nudity as his hands skimmed over her curves, sending delicious sensation all through her body. She already knew how good Zafar could make her feel, with just ten minutes and one hand he'd rocked her world completely. Now, with him pressed to her, his hands roaming her entire body, no scratchy lace between her chest and his, no chance of anyone discovering him, she had a feeling he might truly demolish her world and build a whole new one.

And she didn't mind.

He gripped her hips and pushed her onto her back, settling between her legs, his erection pressed hard and firm into the cradle of her body, still covered by her jeans.

He kissed her deep, his hands bracketing her face then roaming down to cup her breasts, tease her nipples, drawing a hoarse cry from deep within her.

He moved his hand down between her thighs then, stroking her through the denim. She arched against him, needing more. Needing everything.

He undid the snap on her jeans and reached inside, his fingers brushing over the thin fabric of her panties, the touch enticing, the lace's sheer veil adding something to the feeling, making her more sensitive somehow.

Then he reached beneath the web of lace, his fingers touching her damp heat. "Oh, yes," she breathed, resting her head on his shoulder, her fingers curling into his skin, her nails likely digging into his flesh, but she didn't care.

She had to hold on to him, had to keep herself anchored to the ground somehow.

He pushed her pants and underwear down her hips, and she helped, pushing the bundle of fabric off to the side with her foot, then returned to the very important task of kissing him. Everywhere. His lips, his neck, his chest and back to his gorgeous, perfect mouth. She thought of all the years he'd gone without being touched.

Oh, yeah, she knew he'd had lovers. Mistresses. Bed partners. But they hadn't touched him like this. They hadn't wanted to just have his skin against theirs to feel close. Hadn't wanted to touch him because not touching him was as unthinkable as not breathing.

She knew it. She just did.

She could feel herself getting close to the edge again, his hands in between her thighs, stroking and teasing as he'd done that night at the palace.

"Not like that," she said, kissing his neck. "You. Inside me."

"Not yet," he said. "Not yet."

He lowered his head and kissed her between her breasts, before shifting and taking one nipple deep into his mouth, sucking, sliding his tongue over the tightened bud.

Then he worked his way down her body, his lips and tongue creating an erotic path that she was so glad he'd decided to forge.

Then his broad shoulders were spreading her thighs, his breath hot against her sex. And he leaned in, his tongue stroking long and wet over her clitoris. She arched against him, her hands going to his head reflexively. To pull him away, to hold him there, she wasn't sure. But instead of doing anything, she just laced her fingers through his hair and let the dark pull of pleasure drag her under.

Her orgasm swept over her like a wave, crashing through her, robbing her of breath, leaving her spent and shaking in the aftermath. Gasping for air.

And then he was claiming her mouth again, hard and deep, while the head of his penis met the entrance to her body, her slickness easing the way for him as he pushed inside of her.

It was tight, and painful at first. No sharp horrible pain, which some of her friends had professed to experience. But it was still more something to be endured than something she was enjoying. It was so foreign, being filled by another person, being so close to him.

She looked up into his eyes, just as he thrust fully into her, and a sharp cry escaped her lips.

"Are you okay?" he asked, concern written on his face.

"Yes," she said, feeling so full she might burst. "Yes. I'm so much more than okay."

"I didn't know," he said, his voice choked.

"I know. I'm sorry."

"I'm not." He put his hand on her thigh, lifted it so that

her leg was draped over his hip, seating him deeper inside of her. "I'm not."

Then he lowered his head and started moving inside of her, his thrusts steady, measured, and the more he moved, the less it hurt, the more pain gave way to pleasure, discomfort to dissolving and making way for a deep, soul-rending sensation that was building low in her body, in her chest, spreading through her, taking her over.

She wrapped her arms tightly around his neck, beginning to find her own rhythm, moving her hips back against his, bringing her clitoris into contact with his body, like striking a match every time he pushed back inside of her, sending a streak of heat through her veins.

"Zafar," she said, her climax rising inside of her, everything in her tightening to an unbearable degree, preparing for the release she knew would come. A release she wasn't sure she could withstand.

"I'm here," he said, his words labored. "I'm here for you, Ana."

Her name. Not an endearment. *Her* name.

His pace increased, his movements becoming erratic, hard and intense. She cried out her pleasure, ripples of it working its way through her body endlessly.

Then, too soon, far too soon, he withdrew from her, still over her, his hand on his shaft, stroking himself twice until he found his own release, spilling himself before lowering himself to kiss her lips again.

"Ana," he said, breathing hard. "I…"

"Later," she said. "There will time for yelling at me later. I'm so tired now."

"We need to get in the tent." He stroked her cheek with his thumb. "You'll burn out here."

"I can't move."

He hauled himself into a sitting position and scooped her up against his chest, standing, and walking her into the small structure, bigger by quite a bit than the one they'd traveled in at first. "Wait here," he said.

She stood in the center of the bare, clean tent, feeling dizzy. Shocked. Wonderful.

He returned a second later with a large bedroll under his arm. He spread it out on the floor of the tent. "Sleep now," he said. "We'll talk later."

"Will you sleep, too?" she asked.

He shook his head, his dark eyes unreadable. "I don't sleep with anyone."

CHAPTER TWELVE

ANA FELT LIKE she'd been wounded. "Not even with me? Not even…after that?"

"I can't," he said, turned and walked out of the tent, closing the flap behind him.

She lay down on the mattress, her knees curled up to her chest. She had just given everything for this man. Her virginity. Her future.

Because she loved him, she realized that now.

That was why she just wanted to touch him. It was why she wanted him to hold her.

Of all the stupid things.

Loving Zafar wouldn't make her father happy. It would make Tariq very unhappy. Hell, Zafar would probably be pissed, too.

A slow smile spread over her face. She didn't care. She just loved him. It didn't matter if it would make anyone else's life easier. It didn't matter if it made other people unhappy.

She wasn't sacrificing her life to make other people happy. She wasn't marrying a man who didn't inspire her passions. She wasn't marrying a man she didn't love just to make her father love her more. Just to find a piece of security.

She was Analise Christensen. And there had been a

time when she'd had fun. When she'd run instead of walking. When she'd lived loudly.

But she'd let life blow out her spark.

And Zafar had helped her find it again. So this was all his fault, really, and if he didn't like it, he was going to have to deal with it.

Her smile broadened. Two or three weeks ago, she would never have done this. Wouldn't ever have stepped so far off the path she'd been assigned to.

But now she was off that path. Pushing her way through the forest, through the trees and bushes, finding her own way. Terrifying. Liberating.

She rolled into a sitting position and pushed up off the mattress, suddenly not so tired anymore. She was completely naked, but she didn't much care.

She pushed open the tent flap and saw Zafar leading the newly named Sadiqi down to the water.

He was dressed now, but not in his robes. In thin pants and a tunic top, his hair ruffled, standing on end. Because of her.

"You can't just walk away."

Zafar looked up from where he stood at the edge of the lake, his heart lodging in his throat, all of his blood rushing back to his groin as he looked at Ana, standing in the sun, pale and pink and completely naked.

Her blond hair tumbled over her shoulders, her breasts highlighted by the late-afternoon light. So round and soft. Utter perfection in his hands. In his mouth. Against his chest while he was inside of her, chasing ecstasy.

But she'd been a virgin, and he'd made a very grave error. Even without that little revelation, it had been a grave error. But now he knew there would be no hiding their affair.

"I think it's pretty rude to do all that to a woman and then walk away," she said.

"Ruder still would have been staying and doing it again," he said, his throat tight.

"I don't think I'd mind that."

"Perhaps not."

"But you don't want to come back in there with me?"

"This cannot be… Ana, you were a virgin and you are not now. I imagine Tariq will notice."

"First of all, you can't undo what's been done. Second… I'm not going to marry Tariq."

He felt like he'd been punched in the chest. "Why?"

"Because I don't want to. Because I was only doing it to appease my father. I thought it was love, but honestly, if you put your mind to it I think you can manufacture love quite simply. That's all it was. I was told marrying him would be good for our family, and so I set my mind to loving him so that I could please my father. And…and I thought, if I had a husband who was a sheikh, who was bound by this kind of duty…no matter what happened he would never cast me out. A royal couple stays together, if for no other reason than the media. And that's pathetic, and sad, but I didn't know how else to keep someone with me, Zafar. But now…now I don't care. I just don't. I'm the one that has to live my life. I think…I think I started feeling this way when my friends and I went on the desert tour. I wanted to experience a taste of freedom, of something a bit wild. Something not strictly sanctioned, and so I arranged that. But it was more than that. I just think I wanted something more. Then I was kidnapped, and then there was you. And now here we are. And I feel different. I feel like this was the journey I had to take."

"I'm glad that my personal hell was a step along the way of your journey," he bit out.

"That's not what I meant."

"It's what you said."

"You…Zafar, you were unexpected. Unwanted." A

tear slid down her cheek, her face crumpling. And he just wanted to pull her into his arms and tell her everything would be okay. But he couldn't promise that. He could promise her nothing. "But you are absolutely the most important thing…I could never have found this, I could never have found me, without you. I would have made vows to a man that I had no business making them to. I would have…I would have ruined my life and never fully realized it. Like suddenly the fog cleared and now I see everything, where before I could barely see past my nose. And I didn't even know how far life went, how broad the scope. I would never have known."

Zafar left Sadiqi standing at the river's edge. The horse wouldn't wander off. He never had. He truly was a faithful friend, regardless of what he'd said earlier.

He was glad she'd talked him into giving him a name. What was she doing to him?

"I must take you back still. You know that, right?"

"I do."

"I need to see you returned safely, and from there whatever you choose to tell your father and Tariq, whatever decisions you make, are yours."

"It's hot."

"I know. That's why we stopped."

"Will you come into the tent and lie down with me?"

Such a sweet, open request and he felt unable to refuse it. The truth was, he wanted nothing more than to pull her into his arms, her sweet softness against him, his face buried in her hair, inhaling her scent, a hand cupping her breast. He wanted it so much it made him ache.

But it wasn't her status as another man's fiancé, which she claimed she no longer was, that made it an impossibility.

It was him.

He couldn't sleep with her. For fear the darkness would

swallow them both. That he would lash out against her in the night. He couldn't ask her to stay with him because he would use her as a dying man used an oasis. He would quench his thirst with her body, her soul, and give nothing back.

He would be able to give her nothing. He would be worth nothing.

He had to keep his eyes on his people. He had to focus on his kingdom. Wishing he could love a woman, aching over a woman, was that same old weakness, and he simply couldn't allow it.

Yet he wanted to. So much it was a physical need that tore through him, leaving emotions he'd thought long dead in tatters.

"For now," he said. "While we travel...I will have you in my bed."

She nodded. "Yes."

He would endure days of not sleeping just for that privilege, for this little moment out of time where he would be Zafar as he was meant to be. So that he too could be unmade, here with her, and simply be the man he might have been.

A man whose past wasn't stained with blood. Whose future wasn't filled with endless, rigid responsibility.

Just a man who wanted a woman. He looked into Ana's clear blue eyes. Yes, just for these few days. It would be enough.

It would have to be.

He watched her walk around the tent from his position on the mattress. She'd never dressed after the first time they'd made love. She reminded him of Eve, walking around naked and unashamed. As though she was comfortable just as she was made. As though she had sprung from creation, formed...not just for him.

For herself.

She was so fierce. Glorious in her nakedness.

He was undone.

"Come here," he said.

She smiled at him and it hit him hard. There was such warmth in her expression, such desire. She looked at him and saw the man he might have been, and that was a gift he treasured. Something he wanted never to destroy. But if he stayed with her, he would.

She would see.

"Zafar?" She got down on her knees in front of him and bent to kiss him, her hair sliding forward, creating a glossy curtain around them. "You look too serious," she said, kissing him again.

He put his hand on her back, lowered it, cupping her backside. "It is nothing," he said, looking at her clear blue eyes, like the sun-washed Al Sabahan sky. Only there was caring there. Forgiveness. And he deserved none of it. She was too much beauty, too much strength.

"Let me help you forget."

He wrapped his arms around her and kissed her deeper, pulling her down so that he was on his back and she was over him. He wanted her, no matter what it meant for him. No matter if it meant all the honor and purpose he purported to have wasn't nearly as strong as the weakness of his body. No matter if it reached in and undid the years of exile.

Almost especially because it reached in and undid the years of exile.

He was parched, so thirsty for touch, for connection, for her, that there was no way he could deny it. A man who would drink poisoned water in the middle of the desert just for that moment of satisfaction.

Though Ana wasn't the poison. It was all in him.

He shut that thought out, turned his focus away from

the flames of hell, still licking at his ankles, as they had been for the past fifteen years, and focused on the heat of her lips, of her bare body against his.

He pushed all thoughts and recriminations away so he could listen to the sound of her palms sliding over his chest, her breathing increasingly labored as she became more aroused, the breathy sounds of pleasure that came from pale lush lips.

He kissed her neck and she moaned, low and long. "Ever so much more enticing than a one, two, three count," he said, remembering the day she'd tried to teach him to waltz. "Though I found that quite distracting, as well."

"Did you?" she asked, her voice choked.

"Yes." He pushed into a sitting position, her legs wrapped around his back, her breasts at just the right height for him to taste her. And he did. He traced the tightened, sugar-pink buds with his tongue, relishing her sweetness. Sucking her deep into his mouth. She arched against him, her hands in his hair, tugging, the slight pain the only thing keeping him anchored to earth.

He lifted his head and looked up at her face, flushed with desire, her eyes focused on him. "I liked you giving me instruction."

"Really?"

"Yes, I think you should do it now."

"What?"

"Count, *habibti.*"

She huffed out a laugh, then lifted a trembling hand to trace the line of his lips. "My pleasure, I suppose."

"Ours," he said. "Are you ready for me?"

"Always."

She drew up slightly, onto her knees, and he positioned himself at the slick entrance of her body, gritting his teeth as she lowered herself onto him, as he sank deep within her body. He could drown in this, in the pleasure, white-hot, so much so it was nearly painful.

She raised herself up, hands gripping his shoulders, fingernails digging into his skin. "One," she said, "two," back down, "three."

He held tightly to her, his hands on her hips, letting her lead, for the moment, holding her steady.

"One, two, three." She repeated the numbers with the motions, her voice a bit more strangled each time, her nails biting harder into his skin. "One, two... Ohhh."

He chuckled. "Do you think I'm qualified enough to lead this dance?" He kissed the top of her shoulder.

"You were right," she said, panting. "I need to be un-civilized. And right now, I don't need you to act polished. I just need you."

It was all the permission he needed. He growled and gripped her waist hard, reversing positions so she was on her back and he was over her. She arched, pressing her breasts to his chest. "Yes, Zafar. Please."

She didn't have to ask twice.

He put his hand beneath her, on her butt, lifting her up into his thrusts as he pushed them both toward plea-sure. There was nothing quiet or civil about their joining. His skin burned where her nails met his flesh, his heart pounding so hard he thought it might bruise his body in-side, leaving a dark stain over his chest.

She draped her legs over his calves, locking him to her, holding him. He increased the pace, and she went with him, matching his every thrust, his every groan of pleasure.

And when he felt himself being tugged downward, his orgasm gripping him and taking him down beneath the waves, he felt her go with him. And they clung together, riding out the storm in each other's arms.

The desert was still there, dry and harsh around them,

and they were insulated from it, refreshed, renewed. Lost in another world, another space and time, where there was nothing but this.

Nothing but Zafar. Nothing but Ana.

He held her afterward, his arms locked tight around her, breathing an impossibility. He was still lost to the world, to reality, floating underwater with Ana. He rested his head on her chest, between her breasts, listening to her heart-beat. So alive. So soft and warm and perfect.

If only this was all there was. If only he had been cre-ated this second, born from the sand. If only he didn't have all those years, all those sins, all that blood in his past.

But in this moment, it didn't matter. Nothing mattered but this.

Nothing mattered but Ana.

Zafar smelled sulfur. As he always did when hell found him on earth. Fire and gun smoke. And screaming. And pain. So much pain.

And his mother's face. Her eyes. So scared. Wounded.

Then they met his. And he wanted to scream that he was sorry. That it was his fault. He wanted to fall down on his knees and take the beatings. But his enemies seemed to have no interest in hurting him. Not physically.

They just wanted him to watch. Wanted him to see what his confessions to Fatin had enabled them, empow-ered them to do. How the foolish prince of Al Sabah had given power over to another nation.

His hands were chained, his legs chained, his mouth gagged. The confession pushed at his throat, made him feel like his chest would explode. He wanted to scream and he couldn't.

Instead, tears streamed down his face, the only release his enemies had allowed him.

As he watched his mother die. In pain. In fear. As his

father watched, part of the older man's torture. And then met the same fate.

Zafar was back there, his cheeks wet, waiting to be killed.

Praying he would be killed.

And then he woke up.

He was gasping for breath in the dark, a feral shout leaving his throat scraped raw, his skin slick with sweat, his face damp with tears.

He was poised, ready to fight, ready to kill. To destroy those who had hurt his family, who had killed them. And he realized he held his enemy in his hand, fingers curled tightly around his neck.

Zafar reached for his knife, which he always kept near his bed, and discovered it wasn't there. And he was naked, no weapon in the folds of his robes. Nothing to use against the people who had killed his parents.

Who had left him here to deal with the pain by himself.

But his thumb was pressed against his enemy's throat, and one push would end it all.

"I will kill you with my bare hands, then," he growled, looking down for the first time, trying to focus on his enemy's face. All he saw was a pale shadow, glistening eyes in the darkness.

Slowly everything cleared, and he realized where he was. Who it was in his tent.

Damn him to hell. He had fallen asleep. With Ana.

"Ana." He released his hold on her immediately and she fell back. He wanted to go to her, to comfort her, to touch her. But he had no right to touch her. Not after he'd put his hands on her like that.

He was still breathing hard, each breath a near sob, sweat coating his skin. He shivered as the heat in him died out, gave way to a chill that permeated his entire being. "Ana, I'm sorry. I'm sorry. I would not hurt you. I would not."

She stood, slowly, her whole frame trembling. And he looked away.

He didn't want to see her eyes. He didn't want to see her now that she'd truly seen him. Now that she'd seen everything ugly and destroyed inside of him.

Now that she'd nearly been cut on the jagged edges of his soul.

"I know," she said, her voice shaking.

He collected himself enough to find his bag, and pulled out a battery-powered lantern, lighting it so that he could see.

And then he wished he hadn't. There was a tear glittering on her cheek, sliding down to her chin. And she didn't wipe it away.

"Ana," he said, the pain wrenching his soul so deep he thought he would break. "This is why I don't sleep with anyone. This is why…"

"What do you see?" she asked.

He shook his head. "No…Ana…do not ask for that. Do not try and help me when I have…"

"How can you live with it inside of you?" She approached him and extended her hand, as though she meant to touch him.

He jerked back, unable to take the balm of her touch. Undeserving of it.

"I have to," he said. "It was my fault. It was my…it is my burden, one I earned."

"Tell me."

"No." He shook his head. "No. I have done enough damage to you." He raised the light and saw a slash of red on her neck. "Oh, Ana, I have done enough damage to you," he said again, his voice rough.

"Zafar, let me have this. Let me help you."

He shook his head, turning away and forking his fingers through his hair. "You know it already. I told Fatin where my parents would be that day. When they were moving to an alternate location for safety. Because she asked and I thought nothing of it. It was all very Samson and Delilah. If only I had been betraying myself alone. But it was them, too. We were all captured. Held in the throne room of the palace." He started shaking while he spoke of it, but now that he'd started, he couldn't stop, he had to finish. "We were bound. I was in chains. They were not just content to kill my parents. They had to torture them. My mother first, so my father and I could see. Then my father, for me to watch. To watch the strongest man I had ever known be reduced to nothing. A demonstration of power and evil I had never before fathomed."

He drew in a breath. "My hands were bound. My feet. My mouth gagged. I wanted to tell them it was my fault. I wanted to beg them to kill me. I could say nothing. I could only…I could only cry like an infant, desperate for his mother to hold him. Knowing it would never happen again. And that it was my own fault. You see, Ana, I thought I was a man, but I realized in that moment I was nothing more than a foolish child whose stupidity had torn away everything important in his life."

He swallowed. "And they didn't kill me. They left me and I prayed for death, lying on the floor of the throne room with my parents' bodies. I prayed for death." He closed his eyes. "I didn't receive it. My uncle found me in the morning. Our army defeated theirs in the end. But it was too late to save my parents."

He looked down at his hands. "And he asked me how it had happened, so I confessed. And he sent me away. I am under no illusions here. It suited my uncle to tell me those things. He was not the one who had led the rebellion that killed my parents, but he was just the sort of man to

seize the chance to have power if there was an easy way
to grasp it. He told me there were bound to be rumors and
I would be better off if I wasn't in the city. That I had to
leave the palace. That I would never make a king of Al
Sabah. And I believed him. So I ran. Out into the desert
until my lungs burned. Until I lay in the sand and waited
to die there. But again, I was denied."

"The Bedouins found you."

"Yes, it was the beginning of my allegiance to them. Because I realized that while death was certainly the kinder
option for me, it would do no good for anyone else. Especially when it became clear the manner of man my uncle
was. Power hungry, with much more love for himself than
for the people of my country. But I was a disgraced boy,
and he was a man with an army, so my battles had to be
waged another way."

Ana couldn't breathe. Zafar had woken her from
her sleep with a guttural scream and then his hand had
wrapped around her throat. It had been terrifying. Con-
fusing. She'd frozen, searching his face in the dark. And
she'd realized that he wasn't there, tears on his cheeks,
his eyes unseeing.

She'd been afraid to move. Afraid to make a sound. She
knew what sort of man he was, how strong, how able to
end her with the press of his thumb.

Now, hearing his story, she understood what demons
tormented him. What haunted him in his sleep.

She pushed her fear aside. Pushed everything aside and
focused on him. On his pain. His need. She crossed to him
and wrapped her arms around his neck. He stood stiff,
but she didn't care. She stroked the back of his neck. Held
him like he was a child, because it had been too long since
someone had soothed him that way.

"Zafar, it's not your fault."

"It is," he said, his voice tortured.

"No. It's not. Zafar, I would tell you anything now because I trust you, and if you betrayed that trust and went and caused harm with it, whose fault would it be?"

"Ana…"

"No. Zafar, if a child breaks a doll and their mother leaves, whose fault is it?"

"Ana, please don't do this."

"Whose fault is it?"

"Never yours, Ana. Never yours."

"And yet it was yours?"

"I didn't break a doll. I broke the whole country. I broke my life. My parents' lives. I might as well have landed the killing blow myself."

"No." Her heart broke for him, his pain living in her, roaring in her chest. "Zafar, you can't think that. You have to…you have to stop blaming yourself or you'll never be free of it."

"You're wrong, Ana. I have to realize my own fault so that it never happens again…even knowing it… Have I not made the same mistake? I was too weak to resist you."

"This is different."

"Is it?"

"I love you," she said.

"She said she loved me."

Anger, passion, desperation, mixed together in her chest, combusted, exploded. "I'm *not her*," she screamed, so easy for her to do now. To make a sound. To demand she be heard. "I gave you my body, my soul. I gave you who I am, and there is no one else on earth who has that. I love you."

He shook his head. "No. You don't love me. You love who you think I could be, maybe, but you're wrong."

"About loving you?"

"About who I could be. I am broken, Ana, so deep it won't ever be fixed."

"Love goes deep, Zafar. Let it in. Let it heal you."

"That's not how it works."

"Enough water can quench even the most cracked earth. An oasis like this can be here, even in the middle of the desert. You don't know how much love I have to pour out. Don't tell me what it can and can't do."

"It is a drop of water in an entire desert, *habibti*," he said. "It will never be enough."

A tear slid down her cheek. "You think so? I thought you knew me, but now I doubt it."

"It is you who doesn't know me."

"And you think my feelings don't matter? You think me naive? Zafar, I just saw your worst." She took a step toward him, wrapped her hand around his and placed it at the base of her neck. "I know what manner of man you are, Sheikh Zafar Nejem, and I'm standing here offering you everything."

He lowered his hand, his fingers trembling. "Then you are naive and a fool."

"And you…do you feel anything for me?"

"I am the desert. I have nothing to give. I'll only take."

"Don't give me your mystic storytelling metaphors. Give me words. Tell me you don't love me," she said, her lips cold.

"I do not love you. I love nothing, *habibti*, not even myself. I just want to ensure my people get returned to them what I stole. That is all I am. I will never be a husband to you. Never a father for your children."

"But you said you would marry."

"Someone else. Not you."

She felt it like a blow. "Then what was this? This compromising everything so we could sleep together? So you could get off? That's just…stupid."

"Lust and heat. Both addle a man's brain."

"What if I'm pregnant? You weren't…careful last time."

He nodded once. "I will offer whatever support you need. But it would be better if I wasn't involved in any way beyond the monetary. Let us pray that there is no child."

He was gone, her Zafar, the man she had made love to for hours today. The man who had made her reach down deep and find her own strength. The warrior had returned—the fierce, frightening man he'd been the first moment she'd met him and he'd paid for her with a bag of silver.

Strange how he had purchased her with the last of his coins, and yet, in the end, she felt she'd paid the highest price.

"Take me back," she said.

"Now?"

She nodded. "Yes. I've had enough sleep."

"As have I," he said. "Dress. We will be ready to leave in a few moments."

Zafar left the tent, his clothes still outside by the water. And Ana stood there, her heart falling to pieces inside of her. It wasn't fair. She should have known better than to believe there was a future with him. Going into it, she hadn't even wanted one, and yet her feelings had grown.

And in that moment when he'd been his darkest, she'd realized the truth. That seeing him as he was, seeing all of the brokenness, she only loved him more. Knowing what he'd been through, knowing the man he was in spite of it, because of it, she wanted to be with him.

He was strong. He was brave. He was hurting.

But he didn't want her love. He didn't want her.

She dressed quickly, putting on new clothes, not the clothes she'd been wearing before they'd made love the first time. Her hands were shaking, her stomach sick.

She would leave Al Sabah. And she couldn't bring Zafar, the man, with her. But she would bring Al Sabah and Zafar with her. He was in her, his effect on her blended in with the marrow of her bones, strengthening her, reminding her of who she could be.

He couldn't ever take that from her. In spite of all the pain she was in now, at least he couldn't take her newfound strength, her resolve to find her own place in life, her own happiness.

She would leave here stronger for having known him. And with a broken heart for having lost him.

She was fatigued and windburned by the time they reached the border that stretched between Shakar and Al Sabah. They had ridden for hours without stopping, time melting into a continuous stretch that she could only measure in painful, tearing heartbeats.

"I will have you call your father now," he said. "And I will wait with you until he is here."

"But you…"

"I won't be seen.".

This man who thought he had no heart.

"Good. I don't want you to be injured." It was too late for her heart, but even so, she didn't want him to get hurt.

She dialed her father's number with shaking fingers.

When he answered, it was like a dam inside of her burst. "Dad," she said, her throat tightening, a flood of tears pouring from her eyes.

"Ana?" her father sounded desperate.

"Yes."

"We were searching," he said. "Please know that we were. But we didn't want the media in on it. We couldn't risk making your captors nervous. Where are you? Do they still have you?"

"No," she said, looking at Zafar, his eyes blank. "No. I'm free." The word held so many layers, so much meaning. And all because of the man standing before her.

"How?"

She knew she couldn't say. Knew she could never say. "I was ransomed by a stranger. I'm near the encampment where I was taken. Can you please come and get me?"

Zafar handed her a paper with the GPS coordinates on it, silent, watchful. Ana read them off for her father.

"I need to go," she said.

"Ana…wait."

She hung up. She knew Zafar wouldn't speak to her while she waited. But she wasn't going to spend her last moments with Zafar talking to someone else, no matter how much she missed her father.

She would miss Zafar so much more.

They were in a vast area, only an outcropping of jagged rocks there to provide shade. And it was almost like seeking shelter in a clay oven, the rocks absorbing the heat and radiating it outward.

Still, Zafar stood by them, watching, and she stood with him, a small space between them, both of them looking in the direction her father and Tariq would be coming from. They didn't speak; they didn't touch.

But she drank him in. She would have to fill herself now, because after this she wouldn't see him again. Her life an endless, vast desert without him.

"Only a minute now," he said, finally.

She turned to him. "Look at me."

He obeyed, and she let the image of his face burn into her. The hard planes and angles, his golden skin and dark eyes. Those eyes, which held so much pain, so much passion.

"I need to memorize you," she said.

"I have already done so," he said.

Her heart squeezed tight. "I wish you the best," she said. "I'll be back in America. If you're ever curious."

He closed his eyes for a moment, as though blocking out an onslaught of pain. "I will forget that information. I can't know. Then I might search for you. And it would be a disservice to you."

She heard the sound of helicopter rotors in the distance. "Go," she said, feeling panicked. They couldn't find him. They could never know.

He nodded once and went back to Sadiqi, covering his face and head again, and riding off toward another rock formation. And then she didn't see him anymore, as though he'd melted into the sand.

Ana saw the helicopter now, drawing closer. Her salvation. Her family.

And yet, for the first time she felt undeniably homesick. And when she thought of home, it wasn't the old mansion in Texas, it wasn't the boarding school in Connecticut where she'd spent much of her teenage years. It wasn't even the palace in Al Sabah.

It was in Zafar's arms.

And it hit her then that she would never be home again.

Ana dropped to her knees as the helicopter descended to earth, and wept.

Zafar rode until his lungs burned, until his eyes were blinded by sharp, stinging sand. He suspected the sand wasn't entirely responsible for the stinging in his eyes.

Leaving Ana was like leaving behind part of himself.

Parts of the heart he'd imagined he'd cut out. But no, it was there. It was beating. Beating for her. And it was why he had to leave.

How could he consign her to a life with him? A life with a man so filled with darkness? A man who might wrap his hands around her throat in the night, thinking her an imaginary enemy?

He couldn't do that to her. He couldn't love her right.

He did love her. In a broken, selfish way. He would bring her back to his palace and keep her for himself. Keep her in his bed. Watch her stomach grow round when she was pregnant with his child.

She could even be pregnant with his child now. But he thought of his hands, covered in innocent blood and the blood of the guilty, cradling a child, and he ached inside. How could he be a father? How could he ever be a man worthy of Ana?

He looked into the distance, into the sun.

He would be a man worthy of his people. And he would hope that someday she would read about him, about Al Sabah, and she would have something to be proud of him for.

If that was all he could ever have, then he would take it.

He didn't deserve for her to love him, but he would try to earn it. He would try to be a man worthy of Ana's love.

It was the very best he could have. Somehow it still left him feeling cold inside.

That night, he lay down without a tent, his eyes fixed on the inky black sky. His thoughts on Ana. His heart beating with love for her.

And when he slept, there were no nightmares.

CHAPTER THIRTEEN

ANA SAT ON the edge of the bed. The room was large, light and airy. A room fit for a princess. Kind of Tariq, since last week she'd told him, officially, that she wouldn't become his sheikha.

He'd insisted that she stay until she'd had a full recovery. Whatever that meant.

There would never be a full recovery. Not from this.

Heartbreak wasn't fatal. It was worse. It hurt all the time. And she had a feeling it wouldn't just heal. Not when she was so changed from her time with Zafar. Not when her strength had been unveiled by him.

She would be marrying Tariq in the next year if not for Zafar. And it would be the wrong decision. She would be making choices to please everyone else still. And now... now she couldn't. She knew her father wasn't happy about the dissolution of her engagement to Tariq, and how could he be? It was costing him millions in profits.

But he was staying here in Shakar with her. And he'd never expressed his disappointment to her. She just knew it was there. But he hadn't left. He hadn't disowned her. He'd even told her he loved her several times.

She looked out the window, at the gardens. At the beauty. She didn't regret that this wouldn't be her home. She felt nothing for Tariq now. Nothing except for a kind of…affection. Because she did know him, and she did like him. But she didn't love him.

That had been underlined by the fact that when she'd seen him, her thoughts had stayed firmly occupied with Zafar. That she'd never once wavered on her decision to break off the engagement. Not even when she was afraid of how her father would react.

A clear head, time and distance had also made her sure of two other things: She wasn't pregnant with Zafar's baby. And she wanted to be with him more than anything.

She let out a long slow breath and closed her eyes, picturing his face. So precious. So perfect. She missed him, and every second of missing him was a slow and painful hit on her heart. Each beat another punch against the bruise.

There was a knock on her door and she stood, taking a deep breath. "Yes?"

Tariq walked in, tall, broad and handsome as ever. And her heart did nothing. "Good afternoon, *habibti*."

"Please don't call me that," she said.

He frowned. "I know things aren't that way between us now. But I confess I keep hoping you might change your mind."

"Do you love me?"

"No." His answer was instant, void of venom or emotion.

"Then I won't."

"And I won't lie to change your mind, on that you have my word."

"Thank you." She looked away from Tariq, out the window and past the gardens this time, toward Al Sabah. "Tariq, you've been good to my family."

"There is no honor in forcing a woman to marry you," he said. "And no honor in treating you poorly for making the decision."

"You are a good man."

"It has been said, though I'm not certain I have reaped any particular reward for it."

"You could still make deals with my father."

He nodded slowly. "I intend to. It is wise, whether or not you're my wife."

"Have you spoken to him yet?" For a moment she was afraid her father already knew. That he was already aware of the fact that he would have no bad consequences for her breaking the engagement, and that was why he'd been so quick to forgive her for it.

"No," Tariq said. "I will, over dinner today."

She let out a breath. "I'm so pleased to hear it." And then she had a thought, one that might fix things. It might not fix them either, because in the end, Zafar was still the one who had to make the final decision. But she could take care of everything on her end.

"Tariq, our marriage was supposed to ensure loyalty and fair treatment. And I would like for us to strike a deal together, separate from the deal you're making with him."

"What would that be?"

"Swear to me that you will be loyal to my family. That we have your protection. Always."

He regarded her closely, his dark eyes unreadable. "I swear it."

"No matter what. If, of course, we don't mount an attack against Shakar."

He arched a brow. "If you do not mount an attack against Shakar?"

"Covering the bases."

He looked at the wall behind her. "Especially for the indignity you suffered, I shall swear it. On my life, your family, however large it becomes in the future, has my protection. You have my word, and I am a man of my word. But if you would like it in writing…you may have that, too."

"I would," she said, her heart lifting, tears stinging her eyes. "I would like that very much. And the use of a helicopter. For my indignity."

"For your indignity," he said slowly.

Her throat tightened, her hands shaking. "Appreciated."

Zafar woke every night, but not to visions of death and violence.

To the illusion of soft skin, soft sighs of pleasure. To the impression of Ana in his arms and in his bed.

But she was never there.

He closed his eyes against a wave of pain. It was a particularly bad one. Waves like that crashed over him a few times a day, in contrast to the low-level ache that hummed in the background constantly.

He moved to the window of the throne room, the damned mausoleum. The scene of the most horrendous moment of his life. But fifteen years on, and that pain was finally fading. Because of the emotions he'd let in.

There was no longer room for anguish, anger and pain to be the star of his heart. Not when he'd started loving Ana.

Except he'd sent her away. But what other choice did he have?

"Sheikh." One of his men strode into the throne room, his expression fierce. "There is someone here to see you."

"May I ask who?"

"Of course. It is the woman. The woman who came here with you the first day."

He shook his head. "No. It cannot be."

"But it is. I would not mistake her. Ever. I have never seen a woman so pale."

"It cannot be a hallucination, because you wouldn't hallucinate on my behalf, would you?" he asked, feeling stunned.

"Sheikh, do I send her away?"

"No. No, send her to me." Zafar's heart was pounding, and as his man left the room, he thought of every possible scenario that might bring her here. To warn him of war, to share her engagement. To throw herself into his arms.

Considering his treatment of her, the last was the least likely.

It was only a moment, one that felt like an eternity, and she walked into the throne room, blond hair in a bun, her curves showcased by a knee-length dress that was sophisticated and sexy as hell.

"Zafar," she said, her expression neutral. "I came to deliver something to you."

"What is it?"

"An agreement. From the Sheikh of Shakar."

"I see." He wondered if that meant her engagement to Tariq remained intact. For all that he imagined she would be better off with the other man, the thought made him see red. Made him feel like his world was falling down around him.

She held out a sheet of paper, folded in half. "Read it."

He took it from her and unfolded it. "This is…a pledge from the Sheikh of Shakar. To protect your family, as it is now and as it grows. Always. Why show this to me?"

"Because I think I found a solution to your problem. But you have to hear me out. I'm not offering you this to fix your problems. I'm offering it to fix mine. This isn't to make you love me."

"What do you mean, *habibti*?"

She smiled. "I like it when you call me that."

"Explain," he said, his heart pounding.

"Become my family. Marry me. You will not have to worry about war breaking out over it. This—" she pointed to the paper "—protects you. It protects me. It protects Al Sabah. But only if you marry me."

"Are you proposing to me, Ana?"

"Yes," she said, her voice choked. "Yes. And do you know why?"

"Why?" he asked, his voice rough.

"Because. More than a week away from you, and you're all I can think about. Because, in spite of everything you said to me, I still love you. Because you helped me find my strength. Because you are a horrible dancer. Because you don't respect the salad fork, and God knows there has been far too much respecting of salad forks in my life. You made me want more, Zafar. You make me want to do more, feel more, be more."

"Ana," he said. "I…I want so badly to accept, not just the treaty offer, but your hand. Your love. But I'm so scarred inside. Why would you want me? You are everything beautiful and life giving. You talk about what I've done for you, but do you have any idea of what you've done for me?"

"No," she whispered.

"I have felt, for so many years, that death would have been the sweeter option for me. That I should have died that day. That the gates of hell were open and ready to pull me in. But you closed them. *You* did. When I sleep at night…I see your face and not that day. For years I didn't sleep right, Ana, and it was worse when I came here. But today I stood in this room and I saw your face instead of the images of that day."

"What changed?" she asked. "Because that last night… it wasn't me you were dreaming about."

"I let myself love you. And when I let that in, I couldn't be filled with anger and hopelessness anymore. I could no longer wish for death with even the smallest part of myself. You filled too much of me. You filled this place with new memories. And you've made me want again. I've been so afraid of wanting, because I was so sure I was as weak as I had ever been and that if I wanted…I would crumble. I would destroy everything again. But I can't call loving you a weakness, because I have never felt stronger. My heart, my soul…I no longer feel I've left them in the desert. I feel like they're in me, where they belong."

"Zafar…if I ever had a doubt that you were the man for me, I don't now. Because we healed each other. You were the man I needed. It was your brokenness that helped me see my own, that helped me find my strength."

"And it was your strength that lifted me out of the pit."

"Then stop talking crazy about why we can't be together."

"You could have a better man than I am."

"I don't want a better man. I want you."

He laughed. "Thank you."

"You know what I mean. I want to stand by you and help you fulfill your purpose here. I want Al Sabah to be my purpose, too. Your home is my home. Because it's where you are."

"And my heart is yours," he said, his voice rough. "It is damaged. I foolishly gave it to someone once before and saw my whole world crash down. I removed it from myself so I would never make the mistake again. Left it neglected and dying. And you revived it. Revived me. If you would take it, knowing all of that, then I would be the most blessed man in all the world."

"I will," she said. "Gladly."

"Know this, Ana, my love, you will never have to be anyone but yourself with me. You will never have to quiet yourself. Whether we decide to be civilized for a ball or uncivilized in our bedroom, it will be fine, because I only want you. I don't want you to simply please me or make me comfortable. I don't want you to slot meekly into my life. I want you to challenge me, tell me when I'm wrong. Butt heads with me. I want you to be fire and strength. To be who you are."

She closed her eyes and tilted her head back, a smile curving her lips. "Those are the most wonderful words I've ever heard. And you are the first person to ever say them."

"I will never stop telling you," he said. "Every day I'll tell you how much I appreciate you."

"I love you," she said. "I love you. I love you. One. Two. Three."

"Perfect." He pulled her into his arms and kissed her, pouring all of his love into the kiss, all of his passion. "Oh, Ana," he said, kissing her brow, her cheek, the corner of her mouth. "Do you remember that day I took you from the kidnappers?"

"No," she said, smiling. "Forgot. Not a big deal. Of course I do."

He swung her up into his arms and pulled her against his chest, taking them down the corridor that led to his bedchamber.

"I told you," he said, pushing open the door. "I was your salvation."

"You did."

He crossed the room and laid her on the bed, pulling his shirt over his head and joining her. "I was wrong, Ana."

She cupped his cheek with her hand, blue eyes looking into his. "Were you?"

"Yes, my love." He bent and kissed her, a kiss full of promises he would keep for the rest of their lives. "You were mine."

* * * * *

#3209 A BARGAIN WITH THE ENEMY
The Devilish D'Angelos
Carole Mortimer

International tycoon Gabriel D'Angelo is haunted by the unforgiving eyes that once stared at him across a crowded courtroom. Now the enticing Bryn Jones is back, and this time he'll ensure she plays by *his* rules to get what she wants....

#3210 SHAMED IN THE SANDS
Desert Men of Qurhah
Sharon Kendrick

Bound by a life of restrictions and rules, Princess Leila is desperate for freedom—and Gabe Steel holds the key. Enthralled by her intoxicating touch, Gabe doesn't realize her royal connection...or the lengths he'll have to go to protect her from shame!

#3211 WHEN FALCONE'S WORLD STOPS TURNING
Blood Brothers
Abby Green

Rafaele Falcone may have walked away from her years before, and his sexy Italian accent might still send shivers down her spine, but Samantha Rourke is in the driver's seat this time...with the power to change everything for the ruthless tycoon.

#3212 SECURING THE GREEK'S LEGACY
Julia James

To secure his family's empire, Anatole Telonides must get the beautiful Lyn Brandon to agree to his command...but Lyn is more than the shrinking violet she seems. Her steely resistance entices him to make the ultimate sacrifice—marriage!

HPCNM0114RA